Anomaly

A

ISBN:9781695241220

Chapters

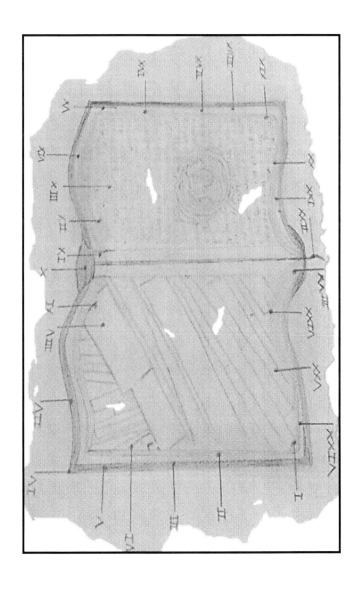

1

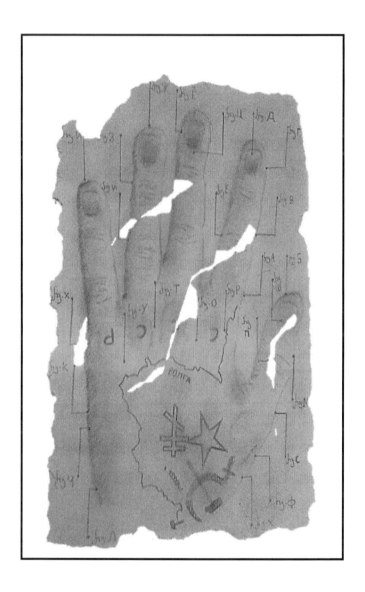

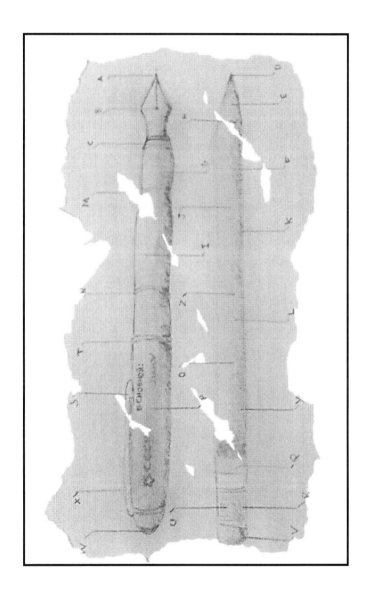

Chapter Two: Burning Eagle

A television whirs on, the sound of an American newscaster's voice resonates from it.

Breaking news just in, an incident is ongoing at the CIA headquarters in Langley Virginia. According to eyewitnesses it began just fifteen minutes ago, there has been reports of gunfire and numerous explosions. We switch over live to our reporter on the ground to discuss this story as it is developing. Good morning Linda, can you help in describing the events on the ground at Langley, and as to how the local law enforcement and federal officials have responded.

The reporter nodded her head and continued talking. *Well as many are aware Langley is world renowned as the place where the CIA is based, this what seems to be an attack has taken a lot of people by surprise. At this moment, the scene remains very dangerous. According to government sources we believe the suspect or suspects are still engaged in an intense firefight, which I'm sure the viewers at home can hear.*

The sound of roaring and thunderous crackles of gunfire echoed near the complex behind the reporter.

According to sources this incident began around 8:00 am eastern time. The local law enforcement has responded by setting up a cordon extending to about a mile. From what we have seen the local law enforcement and federal officials, including the security at Langley has sent in specialist SWAT teams into the building. We believe this is to secure or save employees possibly still trapped inside the complex.

As the reporter continued speaking the sound of the television slowly diminished, as a small man leaning on the side of a table scratched his chin and contemplated. This small man had steely black eyes and a shiny bald head speckled with tiny white hairs. His face was rugged and pale, stitched with many wrinkles and a white stubble. His short stature was more than made up by the strange evil which resonated of him. His dark and sinister appearance almost overwhelmed the brightly lit room.

Within this room hung a large screen larger than the others which encircled the first half of the room. There was a long oval shaped table centrally fixed in the room. Around it were several empty leather chairs and every wall was adorned with copious amounts of Russian paraphernalia.

The small man watched the large screen intently with his cold eyes fixed like an eagle preparing to strike. As he watched, the door creaked open and a tall man entered. The tall man who had entered had a worrisome look on his face, his skin was insipid white as if all the blood had been sapped from his body. The pupils in his eyes were large enough to almost block the blue of his iris's.

The petrified face belonged to Gruzinsky Pavel also known rather affectionately as president Pasha of Russia. The small man however was unfazed by the arrival of the Russian president. It was in all parts due to this small man having a certain infamous name. This man, this small man was Iron River, the twisted sinister head of the FIS, the singular genuine head.

As the president sat down slowly, Iron River turned his body ever so slowly to face the president. He spoke with his deep, harsh and raspy voice and conversed in Russian.

"What's with your face? It looks like you have seen the end of the world". Pasha rose and turned to face him very quickly and angrily responded.

"Tell me you didn't do this"? Iron River smirked crudely and chuffed, slightly annoyed by this mere suggestion.

"Mr. president I have done many things for you and for our wondrous state, but this Mr. president is irrational, I don't do irrational". The president reassured by the calm words of Iron River let of a sigh of relief, but it was short lived. He sat down in a chair at the furthest corner of the table and concentrated his attention to the screen, Iron River followed suit.

They both sat in silence for a couple of minutes with their full interest on the screen. The crude smile of Iron River had begun to turn somnolent and concerned. In his mind he contemplated and surmised three reasons for this event, all in descending likelihood.

Number one: a person with either mental deficiencies or convoluted conspiracy beliefs decided it would be a great idea to do so. It was not uncommon in America for these attacks to occur. There was precedent for these kinds of events. Number two: a person who had worked with the CIA had for monetary gain decided to turn on his fellow colleagues. The last reason that he concocted in his mind was that this was some sort of staged false flag operation. As these reasons whirled in his head, he couldn't help but feel a bit uneasy.

He ruled out the first reason citing that the assailants would have been stopped immediately, given the ridiculous security measures. The second reason would mean escaping, a feat which would have been made near impossible, by the much more robust response by security. The last reason had only one excuse, a precursor for potential war. The uncertainty was making Iron River disconcerted. Very few people, if any, knew of the things that made this man uneasy.

His moment of contemplation was broken by silence, a strange silence. Of all things to come crystal clear through all the noise and pandemonium on the television, silence. The ongoing carnage on the television had ceased, the reporter had ceased talking and the other media people around her had to. The camera had panned to something.

Iron River saw a face on the screen, peering through the smoke and fire bellowing from the complex. It was like a creature from another world. Through the smoke and fire the face had no visible eyes, ears or a mouth. There was nothing that could be made out which was in resemblance to anything human.

When the smoke cleared a little, an obscured bipedal figure became more apparent. It was almost mechanical in nature, but most certainly of this earth. For the moment the world witnessed the being, it disappeared into the prevailing smoke and fire. It was followed shortly by an ear-deafening screech and a flash of red light, in the dying sunlight irradiated by fading flames.

It remained silent for a few seconds before the reporter spoke, by then the demeanour of Iron River had changed. He was confused not knowing how to respond and for the first time not knowing anything. Iron River had seen a plethora of weird, strange and crazy events, but he had not come across something like this before. As his mind pondered, he could not understand how somebody who had attacked the headquarters, for one of the world's most renowned intelligence agencies would simply be able to disappear.

The president appeared to be in a much-agitated mood, he spoke in a very concerned and elevated voice. "What if that thing is connected to us? What do we do"!?

Iron River quipped a reply with a tinge of sarcasm, still agitated by a previous comment, "You're the president not me I just run the intelligence side"?

The president looked back and rather harshly returned words to the Iron River. It was as if his face was gesticulating, 'I'm not a child'. "Yes, I am aware thank you. I'm in a precarious situation as you can see, it would be helpful for you to give me good counsel".

The voice of Iron River almost belittled the president. "Mr. President you rarely ask me for advice you let me do what I want, and I do it well. You usually consult your generals and your advisers". Iron River paused to give full emphasis to his remaining words.

"I'm just an old friend who brought you to power and the only one who can take it away, as I have done so with many others".

The president gave a quiet nod of the head acknowledging the power Iron River held, but in his heart, he desired to rid of him. As the moment of his begrudgement passed he continued listening to him.

"You see Pasha I know of many souls who have vied for power and I know of their cravings for it. Their desire only grows, and this leads to them becoming blind". Iron River scratched his chin as he looked towards a corner, pondering upon a thought as he continued with his next line.

"When they get to that stage, they only see what they want to see, and they see what's clear to everyone. They don't however see the shadows which lurk around every corner, unlike me". By now the position of the Iron River had changed to face the president directly with his grimacing cold eyes fixed with his.

"Take heed from me do what you need to, you know the pleasantries and the charade of you caring". Iron River paused and placed his hands on the desk whilst his eyes wondered to the right briefly.

"The American eagle is burning, and we did not do it, someone or something else has. When our enemies are destroyed by something we know and manipulate, I feel at peace but when we don't, well I feel ... Fear, such a fear I have not known before".

The president finished listening and made his way to the door opened it and left. As the President proceeded to his office, he gave fuel to his ego as his mind pondered.

He likened himself to a proud patriot and washed himself in praise from how much the people of his country loved him. Yet the words ushered by Iron River, dogged his mind. He felt as if something was coming for his hidden injustice, that he had exacted on his own people. Guilt plagued his mind, it was as if a reaper was coming, not of the dead but of the unjust.

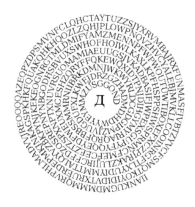

Chapter Three: Violent Week

By the end of the week since the attack on the CIA, it seemed like no one knew of the perpetrator of the attack. The fingers were pointed by many against America's enemies, those enemies were not to blame. The halls of diplomatic embassies were overflowing with allegations and untamed voices of anger and hate, all the while tensions boiled wildly in an already overheated pot of chaos.

As this was all ongoing the government of the United States of America, and their frantic president were trying to find answers. Information through which they could identify the suspect had been systematically destroyed. A plethora of investigations were promptly launched however all of them stalled. It was due to the lack of evidence. The only exception was the obscured image of a figure available to nearly everyone.

The second week since the attack began to close and the third week was about to begin. This week was drenched in violence that no one could have envisioned. The world tried to contemplate what had happened two weeks prior, as investigators in the USA worked tirelessly more disorder was set in motion.

The American eagle had felt the taste of fire in the weeks prior. In the third week came the blaze and the inferno. The CIA headquarters had been left in ruin, yet it was nothing that wasn't repairable. The same could not have been said for the FBI. Their headquarters were gutted like fish, the buildings still stood albeit ripped and burnt from the inside. The headquarters of the NSA were entirely consumed by towering flames, engulfing steel, concrete, glass as flesh dissolved away. It left nothing but remnants of ash and embers of fire, tainted with the residue of human flesh. Grief was apparent in the American president's eyes as he went on TV to address these attacks; the fires of so-called freedom had returned to exact vengeance. All this on a single Monday, the fate of Tuesday did not fare any better.

Russia the mighty bear had overcome uncertainty many a times, but now the waters of death and blood had once again returned. These waters reached the buildings of the FIS, FSB and Spetssvyaz. Whole floors for each one of the agencies were left bizarrely awash with drowned bodies. The integrity of each of the complexes was left uncertain because of all the water which dripped from each celling floor. The Russians and Americans had been left reeling from their wounds.

On Wednesday the craftsman of the legendary myth of double o seven got a rude awakening. The bear and the eagle were left licking their wounds, now it was time for the old British lion. Lions are synonymous for being fearless leaders in the untamed savannah, unrivalled and unchallenged. On Wednesday of that week that theory was put to the test.

The headquarters of the MI6, MI5 and GCHQ were left severely disfigured with bullet holes peppered all over. Some brave lions decided to make a stand but fell prey to bullets from seemingly everywhere. The last rays of the Wednesday sun, which peered through the gloomy grey clouds of Britain gave way to the ghastly sight of carcasses, in a fresh state of decay. The day came to an end, but the week was barely finished.

Monday, Tuesday and Wednesday had passed with colourful displays of violence. On Thursday some kindling of hope was lit to end this merciless carnage, by the rekindled American president, through his words he called for justice and prayed for hope. Those hopes and search for justice were soon quashed by another brazen attack. This time the French fell prey to this new violence, just as the American, Russians and British had fallen to it before.

The remnants of France's turbulent past became apparent in the nature of the attacks. Before the storming of Bastille, the code of conduct for any serious crime was hanging. Deemed ineffective, the guillotine was made to make death painless and systematically quick. Yet the hangman's rope remained in the dark annals of French history.

Through the torrents of royal blood which dripped from the steel blade came forth the words of France liberty, equality and fraternity. Most men honour these words but there are few who don't. These few men made exceptions and disregarded these words, they were made to pay for their tyranny.

In the compounds of the DGSI and DGSE bodies hung like Christmas ornaments swinging in a soft breeze. They were not left untouched, rather they were branded with the words of France and one more line 'introuvable' not found, nowhere to be seen.

Four days of violence, four days of death and one seemingly unrelenting attacker. Words now changed to threats of war, but with no proof for their accusations there was no excuse for it. The threat of one false move from any nation still lingered. Friday was the fifth day of this violent week; the violence however did not relent.

The coiled serpentine dragon of China's MSS slumbered peacefully, watching with one eye open. That was until it bore the brunt of an unforgiving attack. They say when the giant of the USA awakes the world trembles, they fail to however mention another behemoth. The ancient dragon of China forged in more death, destruction and raging tides of blood, than any other nation. When it truly awakes the world blisters, cracks and cries out in fear.

On Friday the world looked on, as that reality came closer. Agents from China's MSS were left in a truly ghastly sight. A singular piercing lance was left embedded deep in the hearts of each victim. Some bodies hung high on the walls of the MSS complex whilst others laid flat on the ground, with the same protruding lance in their hearts. The sight was something to behold, it was like a nightmare born from a sick mind.

As the Chinese lurched one step closer to war, the weekend came. When Saturday arose with the emergence of the new sun, another country fell victim. The agency known as RAW, India's premier intelligence agency was attacked.

The victims of this attack were left suspended in ice. All the corpses were sealed in a face of fear. The frantic effort of doctors and nurses to thaw out the victims was in vain; all the victims were well and truly dead.

The numbers had grown exponentially since the first assault on Langley. The cadavers were in the hundred's now. With India recoiling in defence, the situation became more chaotic. The blame game had already begun, it wasn't long before India's neighbour and despised nemesis Pakistan was accused. On Sunday these accusations fuelled by an ardent few were quickly and cautiously admonished.

Sunday brought an end to the week with the last day of violence. The final attack was centred in Islamabad in the headquarters of the shadowy agency of the ISI. In the office buildings on several floors, bodies were left beaten beyond recognition. No mercy, no kindness was shown to any of them. Blood was left to seep out from the eyes, ears and heads of each victim alongside the expulsed innards which had oozed out. The hot arid air in Islamabad gave way to the stench of death, the buildings quickly radiated that smell and hurried the decaying process. The attack however did very little to ease the bitterness of Pakistan and India with one another. These two nations watched each other's actions with a deep sense of suspicion.

By now the narrative was clear, every major intelligence agency from most of the nuclear states was a target. It seemed to many in the media that these attacks were a possible provocation for nuclear war. Diplomats were fortunately able to see through this, yet an air of mistrust still lingered. The two questions which dominated in most newspapers, websites and news channels was who and why? These questions however remained unanswered. In most minds there was an assumption of a group. The materials, co-ordination and the travel arrangements for each attack were simply too much for any one person.

For some an air of foolish calm presided over them. Naïve of the tense atmosphere they began to call out the stupidity of these attacks. Their argument was; that

whomsoever had done this had unwisely invoked the

wrath of the entire world. With no unity and a deep sense

of suspicion between each nation, the so called 'wrath of

the world' was nowhere to be seen. Some men however

took to finding other means of seeking the truth and

exacting their own version of justice.

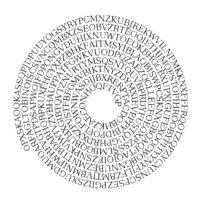

Chapter Four: Tides of War

Weeks had passed and now hidden in the corner of every lip from every messenger there was an anxious whisper of war. The tides of war appeared to be fast approaching. No one could determine where they would strike first, all that anyone knew was that it was coming. Before the arrival of the tide some nations had strengthened their bonds, whilst others had only seen to rip the thin seams which held the peace.

This group as so it had been suggested by many was considered deviantly smart. Concealing their identity and motives added to the maelstrom of confusion making it almost impossible to determine who they were. They were on the verge of causing an irreversible tragedy.

As the tides of war raced closer to the shores of every nations the hapless United Nations tried to keep the peace, but with the build-up troops and the spread of disinformation, war seemed inevitable. A small loose band of people was the only thing that stood in the way.

Iron River was one of the many from the old guard, the elite of the espionage business from a by gone era. Even with many years of experience Iron River was slowly succumbing to the ailments of being old. Although the power of the old guard may not have waned, even as their nooses around powerful men slightly loosened, they knew they could not escape death or time.

Amongst Iron River there were others form this old guard. From them only seven came close to matching him, they were the only ones comparable to him. Like his name these seven had acquired a specific pseudonym in recognition for their deeds.

Of them, one who had met the Iron River in the past was Dark Star, 'the fire of the west' as he was known in old clandestine records. He was an amalgamated version of the best qualities within America in unison with the worst. Unlike his Russian friend he was fiery in nature and his mannerism were brutish. When he did decide to act with subtly it was always followed with a distinctive flair.

His appearance was similar in some ways to the Slav, but his eyes were a fiery dark blue and his stature was slightly more. His hair had not gone yet it had receded from the front of his head. The little hair he had was still as black as the day he started his profession. He had one of those quaint pencil moustaches which ran from the bottom of one cheek to other. The rest of his face was clean shaven.

The last time these two met was under different circumstances, this time it wasn't because they were enemies but rather a lack of one or an unidentified one. Now with the occasional flare up between nations global war seemed inevitable, yet with the careful tinkering of people such as Iron River and Dark Star war for the time being remained postponed.

Iron River sat in the corner of an old coffee shop in Berlin, sipping warm coffee ever so slowly from a white porcelain cup. He was waiting for his old enemy, never did he think he would see him again, but circumstances had led him to seek him once again. As the cold Berlin rain slowly trickled down the café window, the door opened, and the doorbell rang. Dark Star entered and glanced at Iron River and Iron River gestured his head towards the empty seat luring him in.

Dark Star was wearing a dark rustic tweed suit, a midnight blue tie with a black overcoat and adorned on his head was a black fedora, just like the day he first met Iron River. He walked towards Iron River with his long black cane embellished with a glass ball on the top, as he griped it with the leather gloves on his hand. He encroached closer to Iron River and let of a wry smile as did he. He removed his coat and placed it around the chair and placed his hat on the table alongside his cane and sat down.

"I see time has not been so kind to you". Iron River gestured towards the cane.

"At least I have hair". They both wryly chuckled before Dark Star spoke again. "Well aren't you going to offer me any coffee"?

"Still the cheap one I see". Iron River scratched his chin sarcastically contemplating. "Let me see black and two sugars if I recall".

"Yes, your memory has served you well". Dark Star looked at Iron River with a face slightly tinted in amazement. Iron River signalled towards the waiter, the waiter brought the coffee and placed it on the table.

The sound of the café had fallen quiet after the rain had turned into a drizzle outside. The two men sat in a secluded corner as Iron River got down to business.

"I feel as though both of us are need of information". Dark Star nodded his head whilst looking at his cup as he replied "Indeed, both of us are, given our current circumstances".

Iron River replied, "I have accessed my old contacts, but it has been to no avail".

"I have too, it seems our mystery group continues to allude us" replied Dark Star.

Iron River scratched his stubble as he spoke with a sombre voice "Our Russian boys were somehow drowned; the count was placed at a hundred bodies. All of them were experienced officers, I knew them all, some better than others".

Dark Star circled the ring of the cup as he replied in a similar sombre mood, "Our boys were burned to a crisp I couldn't recognize any of them by face. Some of the victims were people who I had worked with over the decades many of them were close colleagues".

Looking at Dark Star, Iron River spoke with dissatisfaction, "Too many corpses, too many funerals and too much of inaction. There has been rumours of bodies in Pakistan, India and China, their governments have severely downplayed the numbers. My subordinate says that they are more than rumours and its worse than they say it is, he said the pictures are beyond the imagination of the mind. I guess I have that to look forward to tomorrow. From him it seems like we have had it easy".

"All of these attacks within hours of each other, what kind of person has the time to do this to anyone? I mean killing a man straight I wouldn't have flickered an eye, but to individually drown, impale and hang each body, who does that"? Replied Dark Star.

"One thing is for certain it must surely involve more than one player. The timing and travel arrangements to complete each attack within hours of each other are evidence enough" Iron River replied.

Iron River raised his head to make sure his eyes were level with Dark Star's. With focused intent he watched the eyes of his adversary as he spoke the next words. "Do you have anything of value? So far we have come up with very little to go on".

Dark Star rummaged deep into his head as to how to reply next to Iron River regarding information he had. Dark Star looked at him with false eyes as he spoke, "Other than the post-mortem's and the type of incendiary explosives used there wasn't much else".

Iron River enquired further, knowing full well of the deceit behind Dark Star's eyes. "No trace on the explosives, CCTV anything else"?

"I'm afraid not my friend" replied Dark Star. Iron River scratched his stubble once more as he spoke, "This is a message of sorts; it has to be. Why bother attacking these places without reason"? He paused before continuing speaking "We haven't got much to go on. Why don't we consider contacting other such sources"?

Dark Star looked at Iron River with a mild begrudging face before speaking, "You would deem this a necessary situation for me or you to contact other such sources"?

"I would not have suggested it to you otherwise" replied the Iron River as he smirked wickedly.

Dark Star looked at the clock in the café and rose from the chair he was sitting in. "It has been nice talking to you, but I think it's time for me to go".

"Looks like our paths have finally crossed, it seems were going to be working together from now on" said Iron River.

Dark Star replied as he looked on with sinister thoughts "It seems so, it seems so".

Dark Star placed his overcoat on followed by his hat and gloves. He gripped his cane firmly in his right hand, whilst with the other hand he drank the mildly warm coffee in one go and placed the cup back down. "Thank you for the coffee, dosvidaniya Mr Zhukov".

"Dosvidaniya Mr Murphy" replied Iron River. Dark Star nodded his head as did Iron River and he walked towards the door and left.

A few minutes had passed since Dark Star had left, and as Iron River sat quietly a memory congealed in his mind. He remembered a man being drowned, there was nothing interesting about the man, other than the fact he was the third man he was drowning today. He was testing how long it would take before a man could take no more. He remembered how that man survived but only just. He remembered him coughing up blood and water, he felt a sickening satisfaction from it. From his point of view, it was just research. As the thought quickly appeared it just as quickly dissipated from his head. He found it strange but thought nothing of it.

He turned his attention back to contacting these other sources like he had suggested to Dark Star. These 'other sources' were specific individuals. They were defined as people like him, just as callous and as conniving as him. To Iron River they were known as the seven patriarchs, Dark Star was amongst them. They all had their traits and quirks which made them more than distinct from one another.

One of them was known simply as the Gentleman. An individual who was an arrogant, chauvinistic, egotistical aristocrat. He often prided himself on being superior to everyone else, by claiming false links to noble chains. His country of origin like he would like to claim often was the UK. Yet he would never discern the country or county, because he was born in Munich the capital of Bavaria.

In appearance, this man was all that of over-achieving minor lord of an estate. He adorned himself in those high-flying fancy suits with luxury black leather Oxford shoes. His face was more elongated at his chin but still very square and his body symmetrical in every aspect. He physicality was that of a meagre man all skinny and bony, but he made that up with his precise and coordinated ability to fight.

As for his gentlemanly conduct it was merely a ruse. Many of his enemies had paid the price for assuming so little of him. His fighting style and attitude was ferocious and merciless or so rumours say. His aptitude for fighting went hand in hand with his ability to shoot. Hunting wild game made him an expert with all matters surrounding guns. He was considered by many a formidable foe, even with his prowess he was nothing but a pesky fly in the eyes of Iron River. Circumstances had forced Iron River to meet him, he was going to utilise this meeting to exert his influence.

Chapter Five: Mystery Man

Seconds, minutes, hours, days, weeks and months came and went and yet remained the consortium of confusion.

Our friend Iron River had met the Gentleman as well as another patriarch, from them he gathered pieces of information which were slowly filling the empty gaps. With these pieces Iron River delicately tampered the web of war with small strings of deceiving material. In truth all that these intelligence agencies and governmental organisations were doing, was going around in circles all due to the interference from the patriarchs. Patriarchs such as Dark Star who like many of the others had made this investigation a personal affair. Each patriarch had gone to great lengths to keep away prying eyes yet not as much as Iron River.

The old Russian was sitting in a dark and dingy office scratching his stubble whilst fixed in a deep thought. His deep thought was focused on the attack against his colleagues. The sight of fellow comrades, who had shown him unbreakable loyalty all mangled, cold and dead was exacerbating his anger, in some ways it was clouding his mind with thoughts of retribution.

He sat there with an unnamed file flickering through the pages and stopping occasionally to read. The file he had, had been given no name, so he decided to give it one. With swift movements of his hand and pen he swiftly jotted down the case number and name 'Case 1: Mystery Man' named after the first sighting of the figure in the USA.

As he flickered through the file some more, he soon became frustrated. He rose from his desk and began pacing up and down his office. In mind he began asking questions about the information that he had gathered up, until now. There were a few working presumptions he was going off, the first one was that these attacks had been committed by a group. The second presumption was that this group had a leader, one that Iron River was keen to find a way to exploit. Yet their remained many questions such as, what were the motives of this group? Where were they planning to strike next? And who was their leader? For the moment this group and its leader remained out of the grasp of Iron River.

Meanwhile the world media was in a frenzy. Every outlet was eagerly trying to seek out the truth. However, many were solely interested in creating hysteria in order to fill their own back pockets. Some claims by certain anchors were wildly conspiratorial hanging by thinnest threads of factual evidence, these claims only deluded more people. As the frenzy continued, one interview made a notable impression.

The interview in question was being held on the BBC between a presenter and a professor by the name of James Nicholson. The professor was sitting in a small office talking on a livestream. He was an expert in psychology and anti-terrorism. The presenter began the interview by asking "Professor in your opinion why do you believe these terrorist attacks have occurred"?

The professor replied "Well first of let me begin by stating for the benefit of your viewers, declaring exactly what is terrorism? Terrorism is defined as an act of violence committed by a non-state actor or a state sponsored actor, against innocent civilians for political or ideological beliefs. In these attacks I believe one of the aspects of terrorism have been exacted, such as the attacks being supposedly perpetrated by a non-state actor, however I don't categorize these attacks as terror related because they don't meet the other criteria.

Technicality aside these attacks are still barbaric and morally unjustifiable. From what is observable the attacks have been against government-based institutions, so the assailants have chosen specific targets, and this isn't a frenzied attack rather a more specified and concentrated attack. That all aside, identifying the reasoning I believe is very difficult. From the perspective of myself it's difficult to ascertain data from such individuals, as often we are by law ordered to give identities of such individuals. Thus, it becomes more and more difficult to find individuals who are going to commit such attacks. But from the instances that we have gathered data we understand that the attacker archetype remains undefined and they can follow different traits. The reasoning for doing such attacks also can vary.

In cases of religious based extremism often the attacker is alienated and feels a longing to correct social injustices. It also very difficult for individuals to leave such groups as there is a group mentally and everything they do is for the group" the professor stopped talking as the interviewer intervened with a secondary question.

The presenter asked, "If this group is attacking

government-based institutions should other institutions take precautions and what precautions should they take"?

The professor replied "These attacks where well executed and no perpetrators have been caught. I mainly focus on advising governments on the best way to precede with anti-terrorism doctrine, this in no way makes me an expert on internal security. My suggestion however would be that these agencies need to assess how they were infiltrated. Once that is known those infiltration points need to be improved much like a firewall to prevent the possibility of another attack. This reinforcing procedure should be applied to key high value targets".

The presenter followed up by asking "Of course this reinforcing as you suggest may not prevent all attacks and not everything can be guaranteed to be protected from an initial attack, can it"?

"That is a possibility that an attack might occur even

with this procedure, in that case agencies should look increasing response times to an initial attack to prevent further loss of life" replied the professor.

The presenter proceeded with a fourth question "Even with such measures as you state, the attacks which have occurred have been spectacular in nature, I mean you have names such as MI6, CIA and FSB and many others, so how long before a sense of relative safety be established"?

There is an understandable fear in the public of each nation. Primarily because of the audaciousness of the attacks and as to whom they've been perpetrated against. As well as the failure of these institutions to protect themselves. However, I believe the governments of each of the countries which have been affected, can and should be able to respond to the current situation with appropriate measures".

The presenter proceeded with his last and final

question "Just the last question, do you believe that these attacks may be sate sponsored"?

The professor responded "I don't believe that they are state sponsored. I believe if there was evidence to suggest so we would have found out by now. I don't think that it would be very wise of any country because there is a risk it may lead to war. I think this group as we are assuming, given to the complexity it is required to complete such attacks... That they are non-state actors, but not state sponsored. However, what remains unclear is who they are? What they want? And whether they will strike again"?

As the presenter proceeded to finish of the interview the transmission was interrupted for a moment. The screens of those who were watching BBC news turned black, before white lettering slowly appeared on the screen it spelt 'BEG FOR MERCY', they remained for about five seconds before they faded to black, and the transmission was restored. This occurred throughout the week to several news organisations across the globe. The mystery man's mystery deepened as fear fermented in the chambers of governments and in the public.

Chapter Six: Burnt Man

Dark Star, the American patriarch for the intelligence agencies of America had long held an inhuman, fanatic fascination for burning things. Through his fascination for his 'methods' he acquired his other name 'the fire of the west'. He was synonymous with using fire as a tool of torture so much, that he was almost religiously worshipping it. He liked to burn his victims to the point they either had scars to remember him by or they were cremated to ash.

He, like the other patriarchs did it for research of course. He had many victims but there was always one, one they always vividly remembered not because who they were, what their name was, but because of how they reacted. Often with experimentation you have those who have died and those who have survived. The more memorable of the two is the one who has survived. With

Dark Star there was one such individual he vividly remembered.

On the fourth of July of two thousand and seven a young man came into his custody. On that day, he was mildly drunk but that didn't stop him from continuing his experiments. The young man was in shackles, he was motionless and barely alive, buried in an endless misery. It was like he had endured a thousand tortures for every day of his existence. There was nothing exceptional about him, he had a physique of a late adolescent aged man, but it was bruised and scared. His head was bald speckled with scratch marks, his face painted with dread and eyes empty of hope. The young man's state was of little concern to Dark Star.

The room in which he burned his victims was a large four-sided concrete structure. It had a steel door located at one end of the room and a rusted old bolt lock the only way in or out. It had no windows expect a ventilation system, which was the only thing that let in on occasion a flaked ray of daylight. It was dimly lit by a single hanging light which started from celling and extended five meters down. The light hung directly over the victim who was about to be burned. In the centre lay the young man shackled and gagged to a dentist's chair waiting for the pain. Next to him was the trolley on which the tools sat. Dark Star had the tools arranged on a tray, from the smallest to the largest still glued with residual flesh and blood still sizzling away. The stench of the room was of burnt hair and flesh.

Dark Star wore a flame-retardant suit and he carried a checklist, he usually placed that on the side on the same trolley as his tools, on that day there was no exception.

He started off by using a small taser which he would use first, gradually increasing the voltage as well as the adjusting the current from time to time. That young man that lay on the chair shackled in chain embraced the first blow, gritting his teeth and biting hard on the gag whilst letting off a small grumbled cry of pain. The blows continued in the same place and the young man repeated his reaction as he did for the first blow. After twenty consecutive blows in the same spot a bruise began to form on the upper right corner of the young man's chest. The procedure was repeated on the upper left of the chest, as well as the left and right thigh and yet again bruises formed. Each time the young man gave a small grumbled cry of pain. After Dark Star finished with the taser he took down some notes and proceeded to his next tool.

This time a lighter, except this lighter ran on a toxic petrochemical of sorts. He brought the lighter close to the young man's right arm and proceeded to burn his flesh. This time the young man only clenched his teeth on the gag and bared it; he did not let off any cry of pain. Dark Star continued to the point where the pain grew to become excruciating. The victim clenched harder with his teeth on the gag this time however tears rolled down his cheeks. It lasted for a minute and once it was done an elongated scorched mark had formed. He placed the lighter down and took some notes before continuing onto the next tool.

Dark Star picked up a mask soaked in gasoline. He affixed it on to his victim and without any remorse he set it alight. The victim struggled but it was to no avail he wasn't going to be free any time soon. The mask continued burning to the point where it was almost imprinting itself onto the face of the victim. Dark Star removed the mask as soon as those signs became apparent. The victims face now besieged by stress and fear had beads of sweat dripping down, in some places small bits of the mask smouldered on his face. Dark Star scribbled once again and proceeded to his next tool.

The final tool was the most sadistic and utterly

barbaric, the tool in question was a flame thrower. In terms of torture, the flame thrower was useless, realising this Dark Star had devised a method to use it without killing his victims.

Dark Star had grown impressed by the young man, usually his victims begged him to stop but this young man hadn't. Even so he was going to use the flame thrower, he leaned to a button which was located on the trolley with his tools and pressed it. Within a few seconds some men with medical attire walked into the room and over towards the victim. They undid his restrains in doing so the young man collapsed to the floor, too weak to resist and exhausted by the pain enforced upon him. He thought that the pain would end he couldn't have been more wrong. The men lifted the young man up and moved towards the door and stopped halfway.

A moment later some more men entered pushing a black cast iron box with a heavy iron door on wheels.

The young man looked on with a sense of disbelief and hopelessness. The door was opened, and he was hurled in before the door was sealed. Dark Star trudged on over to the box with the flamethrower from the trolley attached to his back, a wry smile formed on his lips. Then he let the flame loose heating up the box, inside the young man did not know what to expect all he was hoping, was for it to end.

Upon hearing the flames hitting against the iron the young man gave up all hope and prayed for a swift death. The flames intensified around the box and the heat inside sweltered, surely it was the young man's end.

Dark Star had enjoyed torturing the young man yet understanding the enduring limits of torture from countless other victims, he decided to stop. It was not through pity that he did so, rather it was the insufferable cries of mercy and relief from his victims which usually dictated whether they would die or live. For the young man who had not yelped or cried for relief or mercy he had earned the right to live another day.

Dark Star switched of the flame thrower and instructed his men to open the box. Inside was the body of the weakened young man slumped on the floor of the box, his muscles had relented as a result he could no longer stand. Dark Star's men shackled the young man and dragged him out of the room into a cell and locked him in.

The young man didn't move from the floor and lay there in a semi lucid state. He was awake, that was in no small part to his bruises and charred skin. The searing pain made him unable to sleep properly and kept him in a semi lucid state. Now imagine, bear all that torture and then lay semi-aware and helpless, as another victim screams in agony and endures what you have like a wicked record on repeat.

Chapter Seven: Memory

Memories are things which latch on to the brain and never let go. Sometimes they remind us of the joy of life, all the days you wish you could relive. Other times they tell a story of pain and sorrow a story you wish to forget but never can. Memories are things which last far longer than most, they often dictate the story of your life. For the so-called leader of this group he too had a story written in memories. His name I don't remember, his goals ambiguous, his existence nothing short of an anomaly.

The memories are something which I can use to tell you his story. They began at a river in a small quaint village, one of the oldest memories he has. It was sunny, and the glare of sun shimmered off the still waves of the small river. The water was tepid to the skin comfortable to swim in. There was a boy playing in the river and across on the banks the face of a middle-aged women smiling towards him, as she collected the clothes which had been left to dry.

The boy filled with joy and adventure plunged his head into the water to see the fish which swam in the river. He stayed in the water for a while holding his breath to see how long he could do so. He stayed in the water until his lungs were bursting for air. When his head arose out of the water, he saw the woman who was smiling at him was gone. The basket she was carrying to place her clothes into was the only thing there. He looked further ahead, and in the distance, he could see flame and smoke rising from buildings and he could hear distant faint screams.

His heart sank, and tears began to form in his eyes but before one tear could be shed a man with a familiar face came running towards him on the shore of the river, he screamed at him "RUN"! When he heard the voice, his body became paralyzed, when the man screamed the second time "RUN"! The boy moved, he swam as fast as his little legs, arms and body could towards the shore of the river.

Upon reaching the shores he glanced up and down it, looking for the man, his eyes found the man slouched next to a tree. The man looked wounded by the way he clenched his stomach as he squirmed in anguish. His face was fixed on the boy and as the life from his eyes began to wane, he screamed with whatever strength he had left "RUN"! He hesitated as the question to help or not whirled in his head. On the second glance, the man with his begging eyes and hands pleaded to the boy, for him to go.

He felt guilty, but he did as he was told and in his bare feet he ran, no sooner than he had set off he heard a loud bang, not wanting to look back he ran faster.

Running through the trees and dense vegetation. His heart was pounding screaming to be ripped out of his body. His feet swollen and hurting, and his eyes were shedding tears to the point where they were almost dry, his legs, arms and body were burning, his mouth arid like a desert, his mind racing with fear, his bones aching, his muscles sore and the thought of rest slowly creeping in.

His body began to slouch to one side, he felt limp even as his legs and feet kept running. Eventually he collapsed near a tree, his eyes closed, and his heart slowed, and he rested. He had run on sheer adrenaline for a considerable time and now his energy was completely spent. Slumped against the tree, the pain he had endured through running seeped out in the form of blood. His feet were badly grazed along with his arms from cutting into the brush with his hands. Rich scarlet blood trickled from his frail body as it formed small pools of blood, flies began to circle him like vultures sensing the life fading from him.

His eyes opened after some hours. When he awoke, he saw his hands dangling down swinging in a cool breeze. He was still sore from the pain of running but too tired to express any emotion of anguish, he wasn't even capable of a grunt. As he watched his arms swaying in the light breeze, he realised the ground was moving and he felt a tight grip around his waist. He wondered what it might be, he lifted his head to observe what was gripping him. His eyes lit up with fear when he saw a hand, one he didn't know. He wanted to escape but the grip was too tight. He still tried in vain, but he was too weak. Realising this he embraced his fate.

Some time passed as the boy watched his arms haplessly swing until he heard the voice of his captor which was grouchy and rough, "No point in trying to escape you have nowhere to go". The boy upon hearing this, only plunged deeper into an abyss of defeat and hopelessness. The man stopped, and the boy heard a truck rumbling away. The smell of smoke and petrol filled his lungs. His captor walked forward towards the truck and flung him on the back, his bones rattled on to the corrugated steel of the truck.

For a moment his eyes transfixed with his captor he was slightly confused his captor looked to be foreign. A tall bald man stood before him with eyes fiery green and a stubble which was ginger, blackened by the smoke from the truck. On his right cheek, there was a noticeable scar stretching from the corner of his right eye to halfway down his cheek. He had a sharp nose and his cheek bones were well defined. He was adorned in a green shirt with bulletproof vest on it. He had camouflaged trousers with a gun holstered on the left leg and black leather shoes. A rifle poked out from behind which was fixed by a sling. The face of his captor was grim, he wickedly smiled as the boy briefly saw him.

The man reached for a blue metal box the boy's attention turned towards it. He saw a hand on the side of the box one which he knew he looked further back and to his horror he saw a face. He realised who it was, it was the man who told him to run. Before a tear was shed, a sharp pain pierced through his body, he looked to see a needle in his arm and the face of his captor. His captor showed his hand and slowly counted each finger down as he fell asleep again.

Chapter Eight: Ambush at Bodie

The meeting at the Berlin café had revealed to Iron River that Dark Star was hiding something and indeed he was. In Dark Star's endeavours to hunt down the perpetrators of the atrocities committed against his colleagues; he had rather fortuitously stumbled upon a specific piece of evidence. The evidence in question was a book titled 'The Eerie Gold Town'.

He found the book discarded near a dumpster most likely due to the clean-up operation at the CIA headquarters. He knew the offices well and he knew every aspect about them, including nearly every book. At first glance he thought nothing of it, but a curious urge compelled him to retrieve it. For many weeks he left it on his desk unread, whilst he searched for more clues as to the whereabouts of these perpetrators. With the lack of progress, he quickly relented through frustration but only temporarily.

On a cold October morning he walked into his office exhausted from some unknown work, he slumped in his chair as he twiddled his moustache fixed in thought. Through the corner of his eye he saw the book he had left so many weeks ago. His hands reached for the book and he examined it thoroughly without reading the interior. He hadn't seen it before on any of his colleague's desks or on their person. After he was satisfied with his initial examination, he read the blurb, it was then when his attention peaked. There circled in red was the name Bodie with a date and a time written next to it.

He rose from his chair and took out a book from his collection in his office, the book was an atlas entitled 'Towns of California'. Whilst standing he fixed his eyes on the alphabetical list inside the book, he looked down the list running his index finger against each page searching, unsatisfied he walked over to the computer.

He logged in and opened the browser and searched for Bodie, California.

He smirked as soon as he found out about the town. The town was a ghost town, a remnant past of America. He pondered a while, then realised why the book was here. It was a lure; Dark Star was pretty sure he was meant to find it. He full well understood that this was a trap, so he decided to play along, but change the rules in his favour. Whoever these people were they clearly knew who he was, they were probably hoping that he would show up to Bodie in order to kill him.

After a short while of wondering how he would proceed, he walked over to the landline on his desk. He reached deep into his coat pocket from it he pulled out a black book with a scarlet red ribbon marked with a black star. He opened it and dialled a number into the phone. After a brisk conversation, a meeting was arranged not for him but for the individuals who had decided to lure him. He had decided to send mercenaries to capture the perpetrators. They were going to Bodie he was going to get what he wanted, answers and most importantly revenge.

He had arranged for forty marines and their leader Sgt Major Chris Riley to descend onto Bodie with the intent of killing whoever was there. These marines were well trained, well-disciplined and determined. They lacked one quality, loyalty, in a heartbeat they could change their allegiance if the price was right and the job wasn't too demanding.

They were to attack at dusk per the orders of Dark star from the North, South, East and West with five men coming from each direction upon sighting the enemy. He left five men in reserve in each direction. Like the skilled mercenaries they were they had surveyed the area using satellite imaging and scouting, well in advance of the day of the designated meeting.

Bodie was a former gold mining town that had become dilapidated and abandoned after the gold ran out. It lied south west of Bodie Bluff a high vantage point. It had a couple of skeletal buildings which lay barren and empty, but the remnants of the previous occupants remained and their history.

The arranged meeting was to take place at nightfall out of sight and mind from the public. The ambitious Dark Star had decided to send an individual posing as him to spring the trap. Confident in his abilities and that of which he had hired he was anticipating for it to be over quickly; little did he know what to expect. This all was to be executed just one week after meeting the Iron River.

The day arrived and the plan was set in motion. The snow was deep, the wind was cold, and the hearts of the mercenaries beated slow and steady as they waited. The patriarch of America watched, waited and listened through devices of his soldiers in one of his many dark places. His eyes flickered with anticipation as he watched with eagerness. All the while the sun waned, and the darkness grew, and the wind slowly whirred with a low hum.

The designated man approached slowly and cautiously with his snowshoes through the deep snow nearer closer and closer to the centre of the town. He soon reached the dimly lit centre, there he waited and waited. The wind slowly began to pick up and the snow spun within it. The anticipation grew and grew as the mercenaries and Dark Star watched eagerly. Yet the set time passed without incident. Dark Star growing ever impatient decided to call the whole thing of, it was then two figures approached from one of the buildings. The two figures slowly approached the centre. The designated man conversed with the figures and they conversed back.

Through the dry lips of Dark Star, the words of the

hunt unfurled out. The order was given, the first five men descended the north side of main street, the next five from the south side of main street. Followed quickly by the two teams from the west and east side of green street. They combed each building quickly and swiftly for possible threats, they got closer and closer until they were virtually meters away.

The mercenaries shouted at the figures to lay down they did not comply. One of Dark Star's men approached one of the figures to his horror he found nothing. The mercenary looked at the designated man in confusion. There was someone there but no one physically, after investigating further the mercenaries realised the figures were just holograms and their voices were pre-recorded.

Dark Star understood he had been bested, in a fit of rage he ordered his men and the reserves with the designated man to search every building. They searched every building in Bodie, his henchmen were scattered all over the place. The feeling of unwelcome eyes made the leader of the mercenaries Sgt Major Chris Riley on edge. After what seemed like an eternity every building in Bodie had been searched. Riley radioed to Dark Star to ask him what to do next?

There was a slight pause before the radio's static grumbled back on. Before any words unfurled into distinguishable speech and before the breath of the mercenaries formed into transparent white clouds. A rapturous explosion tore into the slow humming winds of the frosty night. The colours of red, yellow and orange poured into the black night. Riley and his men turned their attention south to main street. Using the optics on their weapons they could see the cars of the south team crackling away in a blaze.

The familiar voice of Dark Star ominously uttered "They're here get ready".

"Flare South, North, East and West, NVG's on, Eyes

South, North, East and West. Range North? Range South? Range East? Range West"? Bellowed Riley into the radio.

In quick succession each mercenary nearest to each compass point responded on the radio "Range four thousand five hundred feet North sir, range three thousand feet South sir, two thousand five hundred feet East sir, two thousand five hundred feet West sir".

The fire crackled and spit as Riley's men watched with anticipation scanning the horizon for anything. Riley thought from where the attack was going to come from. There were limited possibilities, an attack from the North was restricted by the road and two hills, the same was for the West yet they did provide good vantage points. The south was too exposed and would be difficult for an attack. The only possibility was the East the houses and mine could provide good cover. Whilst his men's eyes watched all directions, he fixed his onto to the East. Silence fell on the radio as they watched and waited time as the anticipation grew.

The cold bit harder at the heels of its victims. A whole fifteen minutes had passed since the first explosion, the flares had begun to lose their strength, some had already gone out and the fire from the south was abating. The vehicles in the North, East, West were still intact, the possibility of escape was still there. The radio grumbled back on again and Dark Star spoke, he told them to retreat Eastwards. Not seeing in any benefit in waiting any longer and knowing that the perpetrators could have fled.

Riley acknowledged the order and sent a forward scout party of five men to proceed, to retrieve the vehicles North and then West and clear a safe route Eastwards. He was still anxious about a potential attack. The five men proceeded North they trudged on for a while still eagle eyed but increasingly cold.

When they reached as far as Dolan House (North) the sky lit up again, three explosions tore up the black-night sky. The faces of the scout party were left slightly dazed as they watched flames engulf the vehicles. There moment of astonishment was quickly broken by the blaring voice of riley on their radio "Get your behinds back now"! They ran down main street until they were back where they had started. Now Riley and Dark Star knew they were here and there was no escaping the fight. It was either kill or be killed.

The cold was growing rancorous and was ready to take its first victim. The eyes of Riley's men now more vigilant than before. The call went out for an evac by helicopter but all that came out from the radio was static interference. Riley and his men now had no communication with the outside world, no Dark Star to help, they were alone.

Once again, they waited and watched, as they tried to

hopelessly reach Dark Star. Riley now more a less frozen with panic and realised that they were being toyed with. The weather was getting to his troops, the light of the moon seemed as though it was darkening.

In fit a of panic, Riley screamed "Come on show us what you got"! He looked around and nothing happened he screamed again "Come on"! Again, nothing happened, he let out a final third cry "Come on"! It was then when the ground rumbled with the distinct sound of a motorbike approaching, but from where?

Riley's men looked frantically no lights nothing to indicate where the sound was coming from. Then came the last cries from Riley's men as they fell one by one to unexplained bullets and cuts. The sound of the motorbike grew louder and louder as more men were claimed by the snow. The sound abruptly stopped, and a bedazzling light shone in Riley's face almost blinding him, then a tall slender figure leaped in front of it. Riley reached for his gun and let loose as did the designated man next to him, but it was to no avail. As the smoke emptied his gun a shield protecting the figure dismantled itself, the figure quickly killed the designated man with a single silent shot to the chest instantly killing him. The figure had efficiently removed every other man other than Riley.

Riley reached for his sidearm, but the figure promptly crippled his hand by sticking a blade into it. Riley writhed in pain as blood oozed out. The brooding figure looked at him tilting its head almost examining the wound. The figure pointed his gun at Riley's head gently touching his temple.

Riley looked up; he saw the figure was dressed in black. A trench coat with buttons opened revealing a body armour underneath. It was accompanied with what looked like a utility belt stretching across the waist. The legs were covered in an armour, the face was empty, nothing but a mirror reflecting every emotion on Riley's face. Blood dripped from one of the hands of the figure, blood from the blade that had ripped into the men of Riley.

Riley trembling in fear and cold in his last moments pleaded for his life "Spare me spare my ch...". The bullet exited the chamber it tore into his skin, his skull and into his brain. Now lay silent forty-two men killed by one man who had spoken not one word.

When Dark Star had found out that all his mercenaries had been killed his anger only grew. The enemy that he was facing was smart, more than he had anticipated. His plan had resulted in nothing but failure. He had hoped to capture or kill these perpetrators on his own accord, but his ego and his own selfish interest had gotten in the way.

Chapter Nine: Drowned Man

In the sinister mind of Iron River, rooted deep there was an unusual fascination of Russia's mighty rivers. The vastness of Russia and the frozen wasteland of Siberia contained many raging torrents of cold water. Mighty Rivers such as the Volga almost epitomised the very essence of Iron River. Powerful, unrelenting and unpredictable just some of the many descriptions of Iron River. He full well understood the destructive power these rivers possessed, how they could change from the tempest of streams to raging rivers. On more than a few occasions he would use this knowledge of Russia's rivers to his advantage, disappearing anyone whom he deemed a threat.

Iron River first acquired the skill of drowning a man through his formative years at the KGB. The first time was bliss, his commander instructed him to dispatch an enemy of the state and he did so with ease. Through a repetition of this action he quickly grew curious.

How do you when a mans about to drown? When is that moment where his soul is ready to depart? Is it when his screams become muffled because he can't breathe, and nor can he let in the water? Or is it something else? For Iron River it was when the pupil of the eye dilated and in that moment every expressible emotion of terror was released, whilst the body violently clings for life.

He used this to his advantage so many times, extracting the intricacy of his enemies plans and knowing everything before they could even play their piece. He had racketed such a pile of victims that he earned a nickname one by which he is now known today, Iron River.

Like the other patriarchs his fondness for torturing victims had created memories and from time to time they resurfaced. Like soldiers they did not care to dwell on their killings rather choosing to forget. But even the toughest of soldiers still had that one lingering memory they could not forget. For Iron River there was one such memory, one he could not forget.

He remembered it as if it was yesterday, it was a winter night, the snow was falling, and the river Pechora was frozen over. There were five individuals near the bank of the river not too far from the hamlet of Oskolkovo. The group of five consisted of Iron River, two of his associates and two victims bounded and on their knees.

Iron River intended to drown both victims as he had done so with four others today. One of the victims was a woman, she looked sick and frail, her complexion was that of a young woman. The other victim was a man he was in a sorry state of disrepair, he was bruised, battered and burnt. Neither victim was whimpering or trembling in fear, for both victims had their eyes fixed into a place of oblivion.

Iron River looked at these two souls and full well understood that they were at the end of the line. Yet they showed emptiness and a willingness to accept their fate others screamed, wailed, begged for mercy yet these two didn't.

He broke the ice and preceded drowning the man as one of his associates helped him. He thought maybe the man would resist yet he didn't, he stopped him from completely drowning and removed him, the man lay shaking violently from cold shock.

He then moved to the women but with her the process was repeated many times. It was only on the fourth time she wailed, and she screamed out "Please just kill me"! Iron River being sadistically cruel did not oblige he continued the process for ten minutes whilst she wailed for death and he would not relent. In the end the cold killed her, her death was neither swift nor painless Iron

River made her suffer till the very end. After killing the woman, he and his associates tied rocks to her ankles and her arms, so she would sink to the bottom and threw her into the hole in the ice.

He turned his attention to the man who was shivering, he found amusement in the man's state. He wasn't going anywhere any day soon not in the state he was in. He looked at him closer and saw the burn marks on his chest and legs and what appeared to be gunshot wounds. What a life this individual must have had and what a sorry state he was in now.

Something compelled Iron River not to tie rocks to his ankles or to his hands. Not because of compassion or empathy but maybe because of respect, some may have seen a decrepit man, but he saw a survivor with tenacious fighting spirit in him. But he was in no state to be a solider for him, he was well past his use by date. The Iron River and his associates picked him up in his shrivelled state and threw him in the river alive. The Iron River looked at the man as he floated down under the ice carried by the current, he whispered a short prayer to himself in Russian before saying "dosvidaniya drowned man".

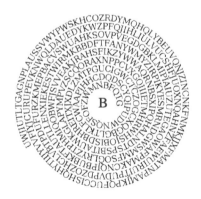

Chapter Ten: Black Rider

A bike glimmered in the cold dying moonlight of the Nevada desert moon as it raced down an empty road. It was going North East from the Sierra Nevada Mountains towards the fringes of the Humboldt Toiyabe national forest. A rider cladded in black armour and wrapped in a black poncho rode upon it whistling past every sign. He was racing against the light of the day which was quickly encroaching upon the desert.

He came to a stop near a small ditch, he covered his bike in a camouflaged cloth making in near invisible to the distant eye. He reached into the saddle bag attached to his bike. From it he pulled out a foldable spade and began to dig. When the earth was deep enough, he arranged his tent upon it. The tent was then covered with a similar camouflaged cloth. The cumbersome armour was removed and the black poncho surrounding him was fashioned into a small cushion. He rested inside of it, placing his head on the small cushion. The wind whistled the edges of the tent and circumvented the cold. The rider was not concerned with it for him the cold was soothing for both body and mind. He slept until the first hours of the sun lit up his tent.

When he awoke the winds had settled yet the cold still lingered. He placed his black armour and poncho back on and went back into the saddle bag and pulled out a small axe. He trudged his way up north till he came to some trees and cut the smaller branches. He returned and made a small fire on which he placed a small canteen. Within the canteen was some snow with a drop or two of a liquid from a small bottle from one of his pockets. He waited and watched as the snow melted and the liquid from his bottle had sufficiently blended with it.

Once the hot liquid had cooled enough, he slowly

began drinking the warm brew. When he finished drinking, he sat idle regaining a sense of vigor from the dying fire. After which he reached into in his pockets and pulled out a rusted bronze locket necklace. He opened the locket to reveal a familiar face.

The face was one that brought him comfort and warmth but also one of regret and sadness. Feelings which were suppressed by his anger to the point where he was almost inhuman. The face was what was left of his humanity and what kept him from losing it. He clenched it to his chest, and he closed his eyes remembering every ounce of pain and the reason as to why he was here.

The feeling of home was growing every day the more time he spent looking and reminiscing about it. The desire to abandon his mission was slowly gnawing away in the back of his mind. No, whatever he had done was right, even if everyone thought him to be wrong, he could not abandon anything now.

He opened his eyes and looked once again at the face, those initial eyes of sadness gave way to gritted stone pupils fixed and imbued with an iron cold determination. Nothing was to stand in his way he was to succeed or die trying. He took down his tent, snuffed the embers of fire and mounted his bike and rode off.

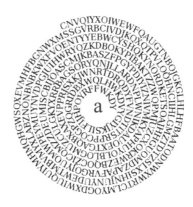

Chapter Eleven: Hunt of Craco

The whirling winds of midnight crawled their way through every crevice and corner of Craco. There was a heavy mist in the town which had rolled its way from the gulf of Taranto. The mist made it hard to see what was ahead. The abandoned town lay quiet at night, but it was to become the scene of a massacre.

A week prior a man known as the White Mountain sometimes simply known as 'the Mountain' had visited the town. In his hand he held a small symbolic patch marked with the coat of arms of Craco, it still had remnant pieces of string dangling around it, almost as though it had been ripped off. He had found it near one of the victims at his office and he knew it did not belong there. Based on nothing but gut feeling and through this patch he came to Craco in hopes of finding answers. Some of the gut feeling payed of when some locals had stated that they had seen some mysterious figures roaming near area.

The Mountain and his men laid in wait for a week in Craco just waiting to ambush these mysterious figures. He dissipated the nearby residents with some excuse to avoid any mishaps. He had heard of what happened in Bodie and was eager not to make the same mistake; he surveyed the battle site and found the best and most strategic positions. Every exit was guarded with his best picked men. Though he may have been prepared, he did not know what to expect.

On the day when the mist came, and the midnight wind whirled in Craco the hunters became the hunted. They had made one flaw in their entire plan and that was the weather. As the mist rolled over Craco it was then the first signs of panic creped in. A single minute had not passed and the first cry for help echoed across the desolate town.

Sgt Thibault a man highly regarded by the Mountain was the first to fall. He was positioned in the most northerly area of Craco with a small detachment of men. They watched as this mist rolled over the ruins and all they did was watch it. Their minds were just enveloped by a sense of stupefaction. As the sergeant gazed into the mist a ghoulish black hand ripped him from his transfixed gaze as his cries followed. Only then did the men switch from a state of awe to a state of terror.

The men of now deceased Sgt Thibault fired their guns frantically into the mist. Flashes of black from left to right made it impossible to lock on to the target. Upon hearing Thibault scream the Mountain gave the order on the radio for all his men to descend on the North part of Craco. The men streamed through the ruins and the mist with their commanders. When they arrived at the northern part they heard and saw the remaining men being dragged kicking and screaming into the mist.

There must have been fifteen men with the deceased sergeant but none of them were there now. The Mountain with his men numbered four times that which Thibault had, even with these numbers he was cautious.

The Mountain acted quickly to consolidate the situation he ordered his men to close ranks and not to fire sporadically. They were able to close ranks but tricked by the black flashes in the mist they fired sporadically. Realising the situation and not wanting to fall into a similar fate like Dark Star's men he instructed his men to pull out. The men pulled out from the town and down to the nearby road.

They watched the tops of the ruins, watching them for a whole ten minutes in fear of an attack. But the attackers had fled, and the Mountain knew. He understood there was simply too many men for them to kill with no cover on the road other than the mist. The men rested in shifts with some acting as watchmen throughout the night.

When the dawn sunlight had blitzed the midnight mist the men went back into the ruins to search for the remains of their missing comrades.

They entered the ruins and a little later they discovered the bodies. The bodies were all arranged neatly in a vertical line in a street. Their faces covered in a black hood; each one was embellished with a hangman's knot. The Mountain walked by each body removing the hoods and the knot. He took considerable time looking at the faces of his fellow countrymen. He took a mental note of each one François, Jacob, Benjamin, Abel, Henry, Philip, Saville and Thomas.

As he walked pass each one, he saw that some were painted with a letter. It started off with a 'D' followed by 'E', 'M', 'A', 'N', 'D', 'E' and 'R'. It continued after two more bodies 'G', 'R', 'Â', 'C' and ended with 'E'. Read together it spelt 'demander grâce' which meant beg for mercy. It was almost identical to the men brandished with the line 'introuvable' not found, nowhere to be seen, many months ago.

Upon making out the sentence his hands clenched into a fist and his anger rocketed. His steel like patience had been outwitted by one thing he had overlooked, the weather, but what made him rage was the desecration of his countrymen.

The clenched fists of the White Mountain soon relinquished the anger was caged inside, and his blood cooled. A thought entered his head 'does he know a Mountain towers over everything and from it you can see everything beneath'. He turned to one of the soldiers signalling to him to go somewhere. It wasn't long before the soldier had returned, he came to the Mountain and passed him a small tablet.

In the Mountain's preparations for Craco he had affixed small well-hidden cameras around Craco. He was hoping to catch a glimmer of the assailants however the mist did not make it easy. After a few minutes of searching through the footage he found what he was looking for. In the misty footage he saw a figure clad in black. A feint yellow, blue and red streak ran up one side of his short, black, cape like coat. One of his forearms was more heavily armoured than the other, his legs were armoured too. He wore what looked like a helmet covered with a hood and in one of his hands he brandished what looked like a white knife. That is all the Mountain saw and it was only for few seconds before he disappeared into the mist again.

The footage did not reveal a face through which he could capture and unmask the perpetrator. Though he had come to understand two things, obscurity was the perpetrator's friend and he was acting alone.

Chapter Twelve: The Missing

A figure sat and watched the dawn waves of the Mediterranean crash against the coast of southern Basilicata. This was the man whose endeavours for revenge were beginning to tear him down. He was the same man that had come from Craco and he had not left unscathed. Physically he had sustained a few cuts and bruises. However, his psyche was severely broken, his disturbed sleep was filled with memories that he tried to supress to no avail. Day after day he would awake in cold sweat with the sounds of screams whirling in his head.

As the sun rose, he retired to his ragged tent nestled into the rocky crags of the Basilicata coast. He laid on an uncomfortable bed, but on that day his eyes and mind were open. He remained engaged on his thoughts wondering when this ordeal would come to an end, when would he finally be able to rest?

His thoughts did not betray him, they retold him of who he was fighting for and what they had suffered. All those souls which had gone missing from the world, souls which could have been anything or anyone. Now they were just bones buried in the dirt forgotten by everyone except him.

The pain, the grief, the inability to fight that's what he saw in those eyes in his head. They all looked to him for guidance, for revenge. It was as if all their final prayers had been for his survival. Every drop of blood which was spilt and their cries for mercy which was disregarded. Every waking year, month, week, hour, minute and second filled with endless anguish. The total disregard for the weak, old and defenceless. These made him burn with an uncontainable anger and an insatiable lust for revenge.

His body slowly but surely relinquished fighting the tiredness and he slowly fell asleep. In his hazy dream state, he remembered the face of on old beggared man looking down to the floor of an abandoned cell, whilst the dim sun lit his body to show all the wounds which were eating at his flesh. The beggared man was chained to two corners of the cell. He a young adolescent was slouched against a wall, too tired to bother with the old man, only wanting to sleep.

The old man raised his head which was embellished with grey and dirty hair. Attached to his face was an overgrown and sullied beard. His throat must have been drier than that of an abandoned well, it had become shrivelled and wrinkled. His lips were to a point where the dead skin was almost flaking off. Despite this he managed to murmur something, at first it did nothing to get the attention of the young man. He raised his murmur but again the young man did not hear, and it had seemed as though the old man had almost given up after that.

It remained silent for a few minutes, the old man was

desperately trying to gain the attention of the young man, but all the words came out jumbled, his attempts at speech only sounded like that of someone who was whispering incredibly quietly. Yet he still persisted and whatever remnant strength, which was building inside him gave forte to the old man's voice.

The chains shackling him shook, as the stale air entered his lungs and the air turned to words in his throat. The first word that came from that old man would make any man wake and tremble in fear "Boy"! Bellowed the old man as he gasped for more air. The young man attention now turned to those once cold dying eyes which were now filled with a fiery rage staring down at him.

"Listen boy, you cannot sleep you must hear my words". He took a breath and continued, "These bastards have held me since god knows when, they ripped me away from my family so long ago that I have forgotten their faces".

He once more inhaled the stale air into his dusty lungs, "I have rotted in these chains for year upon year, they have taken my heart and mind, yet their cruelty allowed me to speak and bellow for help".

Again, he inhaled the stale air, into his now wheezing lungs speaking slow and steadily, "However, as you can tell, my wounds have nearly devoured my body. I have no strength left in this weak body and no will to fight. Yet for some reason I feel revenge coursing its way through my thin blood, but I know death has come to collect me".

For a penultimate time, he inhaled the air through his lungs spluttering out his speech, "I will never come to know what a free man's air tastes like or how it feels on my skin ever again".

His eyes were still transfixed with the young man, but it looked as though now his eyes were burning with a sense of urgency, "Listen to me boy quick, my death approaches".

The young man shuffled as close as he could to the old man. The old man's breath became shallower, short and slow between speaking, as he pulled the remnant air from his lungs, "I have failed to grasp my freedom with two hands, I see hope in you boy…So when the chance for freedom comes… Promise me …To grasp it with two hands and don't let it go".

He paused as he looked to the corner and with one final gasp of air he ushered "Once you have freedom tell those bastards Horace remembers"! It quickly fell silent as the life left the old man's eyes and his voice finally fell silent. The young man looked on in dismay, how was he ever to know freedom when he was chained too.

In cold sweat the figure awoke from his lucid state by now the sun had reached its meridian. As he rose from his makeshift bed, he felt a warmth trickle down his leg. He ran his hand down his leg only to discover he was bleeding. Then the sharp pain travelled up his spine at first, he groaned and grimaced but he was quick to patch the wound and alleviate the pain. The pain gave him a reminder that whatever he had suffered was nothing and that he was to remain resolute on his mission, regardless of who or what stood in his way.

Chapter Thirteen: Hunted Hunters

The snow was falling at the Berlin station café, winter had come in all its cruelty and sheets of white. In the same corner of that Berlin café sat the unassuming and ever diligent Iron River drinking coffee from a white cup. This time there were two men with him, one of them Dark Star who was particularly agitated and the other the Mountain. They all sat there as if they were waiting and indeed, they were.

The doorbell rung on the café door and in entered the Gentleman. He waltzed over to the others in a manner which was neither brisk or normal, but eventually he made it to the table and took his chair and sat down.

"Fine weather gentlemen" sarcastically said the Gentleman. Dark Star looked at him with malicious intent.

Noticing the grim appearance of Dark Star, the

Gentleman mockingly said, "Well someone looks rather happy today". Dark Star grimaced almost readying himself to strike the Gentleman but managed to hold the urge.

"So, I assume you have something for us Mr Zhukov"? Inquired the Gentleman.

"You are lucky that you are sitting here, the others don't ...well see you as reliable or for that matter see you as trustworthy. Alas we could insult all day but that's not why we are here" said the Iron River as he drank the last drops of coffee from his white porcelain cup.

He leaned forwards placing his cup down and looked towards the Mountain as he spoke. "I don't have something for you, but our kind revolutionary friend may do".

In a timidly optimistic tone, Dark Star spoke looking towards the Mountain "Ok and this information will it help us uh Monsieur Blanc"?

The Mountain looked at all of them and spoke with a reserved tone "I think it will help us in finding out how many are involved but it might not help in finding out who he is"?

With a sharp and quick response, the Gentleman inquired "How many"?

The Mountain turned to him and said, "You are not going to believe this ... but its only one". The faces of Dark Star, the Gentleman and Iron River looked confused when he said this.

In an almost refuting tone the Gentleman turned to Iron River asking, "It can't be one surely not"?

"That is what I saw on the cameras, unmistakeably one" replied the Mountain.

In denial of the words spoken by the Mountain, Dark Star whilst shaking his head responded, "No, he must have accomplices".

Reaffirming his own claims whilst doubling down on

Dark Star the Mountain answered, "That may be the case but so far that's what it seems, just one individual".

Iron River for a while was puzzled at first, but his inquisitive nature soon meant he was firing one question after another. "What did he look like? How tall was he? What was he wearing? How did he walk"?

Gesturing his hands downwards the Mountain responded, "Hold on one question at a time".

Dark Star interceded with a bitter tone, "Hold on, you do understand how many of my people of have been killed and not once have we come close to catching this savage"! His bitter response to the Mountain was only because according to the information he had given, he had been bested by one man.

The Mountain countered his bitter response with one of his own, pointing his finger towards him. "Don't you think I don't know how you feel? I have lost men too, at least when yours died they were left alone, that bastard he took my men and laid them out and when I came to see them, he had a message 'demander grâce' written across the bodies of my soldiers".

Slightly tamed by the Frenchman's response Dark Star in a determined fashion responded, "You say it's one I say it's more than one but that's not my problem. One way or another I'm going to find them and kill'em all".

The Mountain inquired "How are you going to find them like you say? You have lost forty-two men just by following some leads, I have lost fifteen how many more are you going to lose"?

The Gentleman who was listening carefully realised that he wasn't in the loop "Wait you two had leads and you didn't care to inform me; did you know about this Zhukov"?

The Iron River slightly annoyed by the lack respect shown by the Gentleman decided to put him in his place, "I thought we agreed that you would call me by the name

Iron River". Iron River gave a stone-cold glance towards the Gentleman, the Gentleman looked at Iron River and smiled timidly but remained quiet.

Realising the tension Iron River took to calming down the situation, "Look Mountain all of us need to calm down, we will take one question at a time and you can answer one at a time".

"Alright I will go one question at a time" replied the White Mountain.

"Let us start with a simple question what did he look like"? Inquired Iron River.

"He was clad in black, he was wearing a short trench coat I'd say just above the knees it had a bright yellow, red and blue streak running up it. His arms, legs and torso were armoured in a black composite of sort, one of his arms was bulkier than the other. He was brandishing a short white blade with the arm which was more armoured. His face was covered with a mask it was completely mirror like in quality. Around the waist was a belt buckle attached with small cases. Whether he had a firearm or not I don't know, I didn't hear any shot's and nor were any of my men killed by gunshots".

The Gentleman and Iron River were listening carefully as the two asked questions to the Mountain, but Dark Star was still filled with rage. It rapidly boiled over, "So basically, nothing is what you have, whilst these mongrels are out and about killing whomever they please, we are here wasting time chatting, I'm leaving". Dark Star rose from his chair readying to leave.

Iron River in an advisory tone warned Dark Star, "Mr Murphy, I have known you to be temperamental but if it's your pride then there is nothing, I can do for you. I won't stop you from leaving, but they or even as or revolutionary friend suggests him are not out to kill your men as a primary mission, I believe they are out to kill us".

Dark Star turned to Iron River, "I don't care if they are coming for me because when they do, I will be ready".

"Like you were at Bodie"? Wittingly replied the Gentleman.

He looked at the Gentleman and responded begrudgingly "They just got lucky that's all, they won't the next time". He placed on his overcoat looked at Iron River with rage and left the café. After a short while the conversation was revived with a question from the Gentleman.

"Why haven't you given us the recording of the tape? Is it that you don't trust me, Iron River and Dark Star"?

"I don't trust you, but my word should be justifiable enough shouldn't it" replied the Mountain.

"But how can we trust what you are saying is true without evidence"? Inquisitively asked the Gentleman.

"Mr Zhukov knows I'm telling the truth very little

gets past him if anything at all" replied the Mountain.

"So, Iron River is he telling the truth" asked the Gentleman.

"Yes, he is telling the truth for now, but I'm sure he will give us all the relevant recordings in due time".

Iron River looked towards the Mountain and asked him a question, "I have one final question, what led you to Craco, Mountain"?

"It was a patch embroided with Craco's coat of arms, so I decided to chase it up but in the end my gut feeling got my men killed" replied the mountain.

Iron River scratched his stubble whilst talking to the Mountain, "Murphy found a book marked with a time and place he didn't go but his men got killed. You got lucky because of the amount of men you had and the fact it was getting brighter".

"It makes no sense why not kill us quickly? Why wait"? asked the Gentlemen.

"We are hard to find, technically we don't exist yet in some way we have been found" replied Iron River. As he said this he smirked, thinking if it is as the mountain said then this man was either incredibly smart or just as incredibly insane. In either case a formidable challenge for anyone of them.

"I think it's pretty clear cut from here we need to wait until he shows again and kill him before he kills us" said Iron River. The Mountain and the Gentleman nodded their heads in agreement, soon after they rose to leave except for Iron River who sat their contemplating his next move.

Iron River knew what he looked like, where he was? What he was going to do next? Were only some of the questions that needed answering. The only thing he could do now was to be prepared for the next attack. Yet in the corner of his mind there was nagging doubt, that what this man wanted was for them to be cautious.

Chapter Fourteen: Revenge Seeker

It had not been a week since the meeting at the Berlin
Café but in that time seven prominent agents had gone
missing. It wasn't until a frosty night in New York's time
square that it became apparent as to their whereabouts.

Every screen went black in time's square and all the
people their stood confused and scared. Then an eerie
tune began to play, Henry Hall's hush hush.

The screens brightened to reveal a character siting on
a traditional bentwood chair, as a single solitary spotlight
flicked on and off in time to the eerie tune. It appeared on
the screen as if he was sitting in an abandoned factory.
Then it stopped flickering to reveal the same individual
the mountain had seen on his camera.

The music continued in the background as the
character reached into his inner coat revealing some
cards like a magician pulling flowers from his sleeve. He

placed them in a fashion which was visible to the public who watched and recorded with their smartphones. He proceeded to flip each card one after the other in doing so he revealed a message it read as follows:

'Good men are answerable by their good deeds; the ignorant men are answerable by their lack of deeds. But the wicked men are only answerable to death for which I seek'.

On the last card it said 'Exit stage right' the view frame panned right revealing something sinister. There seven individuals each trapped like flies in some sort of contraption came into view. They were all draped in flags of countries, with each one having their heads popping out from the top with their mouths covered. Their eyes were drenched in fear as they wriggled in vain to escape.

The first individual was draped in an American flag almost floating between two barrels. Inside each barrel there were hollow pipes facing downwards and upwards relative to the first individual. The second was draped in a Russian flag affixed in a transparent tank with another tank hanging above him. The third was draped in the UK flag affixed to a barrel below him which had what looked like rifle barrels pointing upwards. The fourth was draped in the French tricolour with his head hanging from three hangman's nooses. His legs rested against a wooden board and wrapped around his waist were two wires. The fifth was draped in a Pakistani flag in what looked like a clear giant tumbler with various blunt objects. The sixth was draped in an Indian flag in a clear transparent box, hanging above him a box with a steaming liquid. The last one was draped in a Chinese flag attached in a similar fashion to the first expect the barrels were full of spikes.

But the audience wasn't looking that intently rather they were watching what those individual faces were watching, which were all turned to the left. They were wriggling with more vigour now. Through the left of the camera frame the character had entered. He lifted the needle from the vinyl which was playing that eerie tone. The mumbles of those seven individuals grew louder as the character reached for a lever, the audience looked on in anticipation.

The character pulled the lever and some in the audience gasped and some looked away. The first individual was roasted alive the second drowned slowly from the water in the tank above which filled his transparent tank. The third was blown to bits by bullet rounds which now riddled his body. The fourth one had his neck crunched as the ropes pulled his head apart. His body from the lower half was ripped cleanly in two and his innards leaked out as his remnants fell from its suspended place. The fifth one was thrown around like a ragdoll in a washing machine as his entire body was shaped into a mush of skin, muscle and bone. The sixth was dropped into a tanker of liquid nitrogen, he froze painfully and slowly to his death. The last was impaled with sharpened poles which shot upwards and downwards killing him instantly.

As each one died a few words were revealed above them it slowly spelt out 'beg for mercy'. Then the character looked to the screen as it went black. They went back to playing the same old adverts as if nothing had ever happened. But of course, that wasn't the case. After this short horrific display was done it spread like wildfire and soon reached the eyes and ears of Dark Star.

Dark Star upon hearing and seeing this event vented his frustration by smashing up his office in view of his colleagues. The audaciousness to show this attack to the public and him, as a trophy taunting him. It was as if he was saying 'try and stop me'. Once Dark Star had discharged his anger on his office he sat in his chair with his head in hands. It was in that moment that Dark Star realised the assailant had made a fatal lapse in judgement. Dark Star pulled out his phone from his pocket and was soon conversing to one of his minions. He thought he could trace the source of the video and then catch this heathen who had slipped from his hands once already.

It wasn't long before his minion traced the call to New York more specifically the docks of New York. Now he had had the chance to close his nets and capture him. The assailant had been smart until now, was this a careless act of misjudgement or was it something else?

Chapter Fifteen: Ensnared

It was long after Dark Star's men had made the trace of the video to the pier, that they were now quickly descending upon it. During that time tracing the video Dark Star had received a call from Iron River. He warned him that he was being lured into another trap and that he should set one of his own, still bitter from the meeting at the Berlin station he paid no attention to the signs.

He arrived at the pier armed and with forty or so men. They pressed from all the corners and directions. Dark Star and his men encircled the complex searching each building whilst edging closer and closer to the centre of the complex.

Before long they had reached the centre of the complex, there in the centre was a chair with a responder beeping under a hanging light. The sense of panic crept into Dark Star's mind he realised his friend was right this was a trap and he had fallen right into it.

He ordered his men to form a circle around him as they did so the lights went out. In the pitch-black Dark Star's men watched diligently. The sound of something crawling echoed in the large empty hall they were standing in. A shivering spike of fear raced up their spines as their hair's stood up on end. Disregarding his position and situation he was in Dark Star yelled out into the dark, "I know you are there, this time this is where it ends, with a bullet in your head"!

As the last of these words unfurled from his mouth, mayhem was set into motion. Dark Star's men panicked as one of them was dragged into the darkness kicking and screaming as he sporadically shot into the darkness lighting up parts of the hall. Then they all dispersed shooting into the nothingness as they raced for the exits. Yet Dark Star stood still watching the pandemonium eagerly waiting for a clear shot.

Some of Dark Star's men found him, knowing that he was the one who was paying them, they dragged him out of the maelstrom towards the exit of the pier complex. From the forty or so men only ten had come out unscathed. They rested halfway down West twenty first street as Dark Star contemplated his next manoeuvre.

Meanwhile in the hall the assailant emerged from the dark as some of the lights slowly flickered on. The hall resembled an art expose, except it was one filled with spatters of blood and bodies. All but one of Dark Star's men had survived. That last man stared down the barrel of his rifle directly at the assailant's back with steely determination. He said something to the assailant which made him hesitate for moment "Was it worth it"? He looked back at the sole man who then let lose his entire magazine.

As the last casings from his bullets fell, he looked to see if he had killed the assailant, yet there was no one in his immediate vicinity. He looked around the hall and saw the figure clad in black face down presumably dead he approached with no due diligence. Therein he made a mistake, confident that he had killed the assailant he walked away. It was then the assailant rose up, the survivor had heard him, but it was too late. A flash of light followed by darkness ended his life.

Outside the pier and on the street the surviving men and Dark Star heard the gunshots echo in the surroundings. It wasn't long before they made the judgement to withdraw deeper into Manhattan. They entered their cars in which they had arrived in and drove away from the scene. Dark Star unwilling to relent decided to regroup at a building he owned near the Madison square park.

The assailant exited the pier complex and took off on his bike hidden in a nearside bush. But by now the sounds of gunshots had alerted the locals and it wasn't long before the sounds of the police and their sirens of blue were encroaching upon him. He managed to gain a fair distance between him and the few cop cars chasing him. He was heading north on twelfth avenue but veered right, hurtling down it. The bike and rider went down West fifty second street veering North on eighth avenue and rode past Columbus circle, heading straight into Central park. There he could hide or find a way out whilst there weren't many police cars chasing him.

Unbeknownst to the police they were chasing shadows. The assailant had managed to the lure the police away by using a diversionary bike with a holographic projection of a rider, controlled by him remotely. The bike rode around for a bit before crashing and disappearing into the Hudson river, a few miles away from the reported shooting. The police huddled around the river searching for hours for the bike but to no avail. As it was night and the river incredibly murky from the disturbed silt and sediments made it difficult to see.

Dark Star rapidly realised the mess he had created and the possible intrusive intervention by authorities, so he instructed his men to divert the authorities. He ordered them to burn the pier and remove the bodies quickly. They burnt the pier complex and just barely managed to remove the bodies away from prying eyes.

To Dark Star it appeared that he had side-tracked the authorities well enough. The threat however remained, so long as it stayed dark. So, when the night rolled into day Dark Star let of a sigh of relief in his safe house. He knew the assailant would not dare attack in board daylight with the risk of being exposed. For the second time he had been duped and understood that he was indeed now going to either kill or be killed by the assailant.

Chapter Sixteen: Shot and Caught

The police and state officials were still in a state of confusion, they were still trying to work out from where the gunshots came from. The fire at the pier and search for an unidentified suspect more than kept them busy. By now the news of the fire and reported shooting was the leading headline, in local TV channels and national news channels.

Whilst the city police and state officials remained occupied Dark Star concocted his next move. He had not grown accustomed to being hunted everything that he did he always had the advantage. In this city nothing was going to be easy, the assailant was somewhere here he just had to find him. Dark Star angered by his latest setback was entrenched in a state of paranoia.

When the last of the sun was disappearing from the horizon and the night entered again, he and his reinforced crew began scouring the city in the deep night. He knew that the assailant could have escaped and there was no guarantee that he would find anything. His intuition and experience made him feel as though the assailant was still in the city. Yet the risk of being entrapped again was plaguing on his mind.

They searched the city in their cars hoping that they could bait the assailant out. It was not long before the decision was made to exit their cars and begin the baiting on foot. Dark Star's men had concealed their weapons in order not to be stopped by the increased police presence. They did everything to withdraw their attention from the police like changing their attire and their movements. Little did that matter, because high above them watching from the skyscrapers was the assailant.

Dark Star kept regular checks on the radio with his men checking on their positions and progress. It must have been early morning when Dark Star did another check, he called one of his crews in Korea town near West thirty third street and they did not respond. He called again and there was no response, upon hearing no answer he ordered his men to Korea town. His car raced down the streets passing each building until they reached the place where those men were last positioned.

He stepped out of his car frantically searching for them, until he stumbled upon their walkie talkies attached to a pole with a note it read, *'you are in my pen and you are cornered, don't look up'*. Tired of constant toying he scrunched up the paper and looked up. At first, he saw nothing but quickly he realised, he was exactly where the assailant wanted him.

The first shot fired from somewhere he couldn't pinpoint instantly killing one his men. The next bullets came in quick succession knocking his men out one by one. Dark Star frantically searched the surroundings looking for the shooter whilst also looking for cover.

After most of his men had been killed it went eerily quiet. Dark Star knowing this was going nowhere decided to foolishly antagonize the shooter, "You piece of shit you should have killed me when you had the chance. Now you are just running down time you don't have. I can bring more men and eventually we will get you… Look at you, you won't even face me, hiding like you have done since we began looking for you. If you are so fearless then face me". Dark Star looked to the remainder of his men taking cover. Crumpling his mouth and nodding his head as if to say, 'that didn't work'.

The wind began to howl as a loud foghorn bellowed in the area. He and his men looked up as a figure hurtled its way down the Empire state building at astonishing speed. Dark Star and his men opened fire smashing the windows, as the figure came hurling towards the ground. Without warning there was a sudden bang as smoke ballooned just in front of Dark Star. He signalled his men to move in, a wry smile appeared had he finally got him. Had he killed the being terrorizing him for so long?

The men slowly came closer and closer, until through the smoke burst forth the assailant with his guns fixed to Dark Star's men. This time the face of the assailant had two piercing, wicked, red LED eyes bearing down with rage. The bullets knocked his men dead so fast that Dark Star barely had time to react. The black cladded figure approached Dark Star firing indiscriminately at his car as he ducked for cover. One of the bullets pierced his shoulder another crippling his leg. The blood came oozing out in its thick viscous form. He managed to get into the car returning the fire as he quickly reversed it and sped off.

The remainder of Dark Stars men emptied their magazines as the assailant ducked and dived knocking every one of the remaining minions out. Eventually he had killed them all. The assailant stood frustrated knowing Dark Star had escaped again but he knew he was wounded, and he wouldn't get that far.

In the maelstrom the assailant had failed to foresee the arrival of the police. Soon enough police officers poured out from trucks, heavily armoured and with their guns trained on the assailant.

He quickly threw his gun in a storm drain on the side and placed his hands on his head. The red menacing eyes had now turned into a yellow smiling face. The assailant dropped to his knees as the police began to encircle him and scream orders. He was quickly subdued and handcuffed.

It wasn't long before the assailant was in the back of an armoured truck, they didn't remove his mask or his armour unsure of how to. He was sitting tightly between heavily armoured swat team members. The truck drove towards the nearby police station whilst everyone in the truck remained silent.

Dark Star was badly injured but had escaped alive and had made his way to the safe house from their he called one of his associates. He was watching the news as it was unfolding whilst his associate operated without anaesthetic. He saw the bodies of his men littered across the street like common garbage. Then he heard the newscaster mention that 'a suspected shooter had been captured'. Upon hearing this he was almost elated with joy surely, now, he could have his vengeance.

Chapter Seventeen: Supernova

A whole day had passed since the events in Korea town and it was night once more. The bodies near the empire state building had now become a scene for criminal investigations, beside that there was now a growing media circus. The authorities not content with leaving the suspect in a local station had decided to move him. There was a great deal of confusion as to who was going to interrogate him first, after a short while of deliberations it was decided the FBI would interrogate him first.

Whilst handcuffed and still with his armour and mask on the assailant waited in his cell. Soon enough he was removed from his cell, escorted by eight armed guards and an FBI agent to an armoured truck heading towards the FBI building in New York City.

In the safe house Dark Star sat on a bed hooked up to heavy painkillers and several medical devices. The wound to the shoulder was far more serious than the leg. His associate had managed to stem the bleeding and close the gaping holes in his skin with stitches. Yet he was still in pain even with the heavy painkillers.

He was now contemplating a plan on as how to wrestle control over the assailant from the police. He was watching the news when an idea came into his head. The newscaster was talking about the events and mentioned that the suspect had been taken into custody, the only question was, where was he being held? It wasn't long before Dark Star was on the phone looking for old contacts until he stumbled upon an old friend who worked for the FBI in New York.

His relationship with this friend was questionable, they had grown apart from Dark Star's arbitrary interrogation techniques. His friends name was special agent Ramirez and luckily for him he was in New York working as an active agent on the case that he was an intrinsic part of. Yet the problem remained as to finding out as to how to convince him in to revealing the place where they were holding him.

He called another one of his associates in attempt to find Ramirez by locating where his phone was, from that he was hoping to be able to find out where the shooter was being held. It wasn't long after that call that Dark Star rang Ramirez, the conversation was nothing what Dark Star hoped it was going to be.

It didn't start like he had wanted, Ramirez was still bitter, and it reflected in his voice when he spoke to Dark Star. When Ramirez heard his phone ringing, he looked at the number and chuffed answered it, followed by this response, "What do you want you sack of shit"?

Dark Star treaded carefully in order to make sure he had a lock on his location "Is that how you treat an old friend"?

The response was bitter and resentful "I am not your

friend not even in the loosest meaning of the term". He sighed as rubbed his head with his index and middle finger… "Look if you want something just say so if not piss off".

Dark Star approached with a more forward tone, as the tone of Ramirez was growing impatient and he had no time to waver with Ramirez, "Are you working on this New York case"?

Ramirez was walking inside some sort of jail with his phone in one hand next to his ear and a file in the other, Ramirez responded "Why do you care"?

Dark Star cautiously responded, "Just wondering if I could help that's all".

Ramirez responded in an agitated way as he approached a cell "The last persons help I want is yours so, if you don't mind, I got something to do". He slammed his phone shut cutting the conversation.

Dark Star looked to his phone and he had received a

text message from his associate with a lock on Ramirez's phone. It wasn't long before Dark star hobbled out of bed removing the many devices attached to him against the wishes of his associate. He put on his clothes and was on his way to the location.

Ramirez had been given orders to remove the shooter and take him to be interrogated at the FBI building in New York City. He came into the cell where the suspect was being held and handcuffed. He instructed four armed officers into the cell as two of them assisted in placing ankle chains around his legs. They then removed the suspect from the cell and four more armed men followed him out to the armoured car.

Ramirez was to lead the convoy to the FBI building, he waited for a while for the convoy to get going. Soon the assailant was in the back of an armoured truck with eight armed officers as they made their way down to the FBI building.

Dark Star arrived at the local precinct bandaged at the arm and leg, only to discover that the suspect had been moved to the FBI building. Dark Star reconfigured himself and headed towards the FBI building. He had managed to catch the convoy and gained entry to the building by using his credentials. Yet it could not bring him close enough to the man he wanted.

The suspect was removed from the armoured and taken to a secure interrogation room. He was shackled once again, whilst Ramirez went in search of another senior officer to assist him in the interrogation. It wasn't long before they had returned, but unbeknownst to them he had loosened one of his handcuffs and was just waiting.

When Ramirez and his colleague sat down, he quickly grabbed the recording device and smashed it against one of them. Ramirez reached for his gun but was quickly disarmed and knocked out by the butt of his own gun. Moving swiftly, he exited the interrogation room but the armed guards standing outside spotted him and opened fire, he managed to jump from the top floor rolling out into a run as bullets ripped past him.

Dark Star, who was by the entrance, spotted him and discreetly exited the building and gave chase in his own car. The assailant knew he was being followed and he had a good idea as to who was following him. Dark Star let of sporadic shots to kill his tormenting attacker. As he ran and Dark Star chased in his car the assailant lured him into Seward park where he had hidden a stash of weapons. Dark Star attempted to crash his car into the assailant narrowly missing him. He tried again and knocked him cleanly into the park, the assailant fortunately was knocked close to his stash, he reached into the stash.

Dark Star exited the car and walked towards him as he staggered upwards. With as much venom as he could muster, he yelled "This is where it ends buddy, this is where you die"! The red eyes of the assailant flickered on, Dark released bullet after bullet onto the assailant as he raced towards him. The bullets marginally slowed him down and soon enough Dark Star's bullets had finished by then it was too late. A quick flash of a white blade cut open Dark Star's stomach as the acids burned his flesh. In a fleeting sense of despair Dark Star asked him, "Why won't you die"? There was no reply and then a second swipe cleanly cut the head of Dark Star ending him once and for all.

The assailant looked at the head with an animalistic anger. He mashed the head removing any semblance to identify Dark Star as well as the fingers, before setting fire to him with a lighter from his weapon stash.

As the sirens approached, he quickly ran South East and dived straight into the East river, disappearing into the murky depths.

Chapter Eighteen: Fear

News of Dark Star's death spread like wildfire into the land of always winter, the Brittonic coast and the Gallic heartland. Iron River's theory had become reality, the assailant was indeed coming after them. A strange fear had now gripped the Gentleman and his counterpart the White Mountain, for some reason Iron River was not gripped by it, he was rather curious than afraid.

Dark Star's incapacity to control his anger had led him to his own death, that is what went through Iron River's head. Yet now everything was public, and it wasn't going to be long before he and the other patriarchs were going to be caught. They all grew distant from one another in the hopes of avoiding being caught or for that matter being killed.

Unbeknownst to them however someone was on their trail it was Ramirez who had woken up from a long slumber courtesy of the assailant. After a short while he was on the case again, he retraced his footsteps and eventually working with his colleague they found Dark Star's body in the park. When he found it at first, he didn't know who it was because the corpse had its face mashed, as well as it fingers. Upon closer inspection of the body he realised who it was, but he kept it a secret knowing that this was something bigger than he knew of. The investigation now turned into a manhunt but for Ramirez it had expanded into something more.

You could have argued everyone in New York was gripped with fear. The bodies near the Empire State building had been removed. Each one had their faces badly damaged and there was no way of identifying them other than the means of DNA and Fingerprints which came out blank.

Ramirez had his hands full, but the White Mountain and the Gentleman had it worse. Public scrutiny was growing and there was a concern in the security community. Everyone in the major European security agencies were in fear of a similar event occurring in Europe just like in New York. The Gentleman had increased his own protection in fear of an imminent attack from the assailant, whilst the White Mountain was waiting and ready to retaliate at a moment's notice. For some diabolical reason Iron River wanted the other European patriarchs to be killed, knowing that he could benefit from their deaths.

The Iron River a Master of Information had contacts in so many places you would think that he was running his own agency inside an agency, and such was the case with him. He had learnt from his minions in the US that Dark Star had his faced mashed in and that the assailant had escaped from FBI custody. He began to paint a picture of the assailant from all the information that he had gathered, this man who remained an enigma, a riddle, an anomaly.

He knew that he wore armour and was a well trained in both marksmanship and hand to hand combat. He also knew from the previous encounters that he could escape when cornered and a man who lurked under a veil of shadows. He saw him as an individual who was resentful and angry against him and other patriarchs based on the way he had killed Dark Star. Yet he also understood that he knew all of them somehow personally even, as if he had been studying them and understanding their weaknesses for years on end. He pondered as he sat in his office wondering if he had ever met him before or if the others had.

He had no time waste musing as his subordinates had informed him that Ramirez had been called by Dark Star. This was certainly going to unravel the strings in their carefully woven history and destroy everything that he had done. The Gentleman and the White Mountain were not aware of this and Iron River kept it this way as he did not trust any of them that much.

The White Mountain was sitting in Napoleons tomb reminiscing about the days of Napoleon and the grand armee. He contemplated his next move with the utmost care for Dark Star was dead and he may be next; he knew that his day was coming but was that day now or a way away. The death of Dark Star instilled within in him an essence of Caution. He realized that the approach of anger was not going to help. He had to be subtle and to not let his bloodlust envelop him.

Meanwhile the Gentleman was beefing up his security taking the cautious and anxious way of dealing with his impending demise. It wasn't to say that he wasn't impressed as to how much this single individual had killed. It gave him both a sense of awe and fear of his determination against such overwhelming odds.

The remaining patriarchs had not been troubled as

they were in confusion as to who attacked their bases. The Pakistani's were entangled in a serious diplomatic dispute with India both sides blaming each other for the attacks. Their media shows pointing fingers at each other and questioning whether they should go to war. But two wise men in the darkness knew that neither country had engaged in such violent warfare. One went by the name of Broken Crescent the other by the name of Frozen Claw neither of them had any idea as to who this had done yet it did not stop them from torturing the innocent.

The penultimate patriarch was the Jade Dragon she was the only one whose very existence as a patriarch was known by only one and that was Iron River. There was an unwritten alliance between the two, they often exchanged information with each other unbeknownst to the other patriarchs. In this case however Iron River had purposefully neglected to give necessary information regarding the events surroundings Dark Star's death, but the Jade Dragon was well informed for she too had

pawns of her own. It seemed now that they were more

suspicious of each other. This hindered the answer to the

question most of them were trying to find out, who is he?

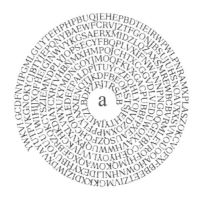

Chapter Nineteen: The Shot Man

The memories faded in and out of the Gentleman's head as the whiskey stench from his mouth leaked out. He reminisced about all the cruel things he had done, and he wondered whether they had been worth the effort.

Unlike the other patriarchs he had a cruel and inhuman taste for unpleasant and unwarranted torture. The torture was entirely unnecessary and unjustifiable. There was no scientific purpose it was just his sadistic fantasies which propelled him to do it again and again.

It was something out of a horror book, he would stand rather arrogantly with his rifle staring down his long estate garden. Then he would walk slowly down each one of the stone steps which led to the to the place where he would normally display his heritage cars. In every instance he walked down the stone steps with his rifle he was always outfitted in a tweed hunting suit, and before him there would be four cages evenly spaced. Within them there was always four decrepit soul looking for some respite. Every time he passed by them, he greeted them by tipping his hunting hat to each soul.

When he passed by, he walked back up the stone steps on the left eventually reaching the wall which overlooked them. He took aim and waited, then like clockwork a siren sounded, the cages emptied and like new fawn which had entered the world, the victims hopped, skipped and ran. It seemed stupid why run when there was man staring down the scope of rifle ready to shoot.

Therein lied the conundrum to run or not. In a true sadists mind, like the Gentleman the rules of the hunt were brutally simple. If no one ran one of them would die via Russian roulette but the real evil would happen if they did run. They would of course be shot but they would not die. The decrepit souls in cage understood this and for some of them running and getting shot was better than staying in the cage.

Such was the despicable nature of the Gentleman he never let them die too easily. He would always shoot rubber coated steel bullets which were extremely painful and usually brought down most men. Sometimes he would use frangible bullets which would shatter upon impact, causing significant damage to the skin and bone but in a manner which neither killed them nor lightly maimed them.

In some cases, he would deliberately miss the person furthest from the rest and allow him to reach the gate filling him with false promises of freedom, before killing them with a full metal jacket. Those who were injured were quickly nursed back to health and the process went on and on, till the victim played the Russian roulette.

There was an instance where one such man came into his control; he was a man with many scars and wounds.

When the Gentleman received individuals, he often become inquisitive and questions such as to where they came from? What their name was? Were some of the things he asked. In the case with the man with many scars he asked him these questions, but he remained dumb to all of them not answering any of them.

It wasn't long before the Gentleman took a liking towards the man with many scars and wounds. The first day he was told to run he refused to move from his cage. The Gentleman in a disgruntled voice said to the man "My friend this is not the way we play the game".

He looked at him with displeasure and the man ignored him "If you don't like this game, we will play the game no one likes to play. Come on don't be a spoilt sport". His words did little to sway him to speak or for him to conform to play his dastardly game.

Consequently, the Gentleman resorted to playing Russian roulette he started with the cage furthest from the man. He carried a five-shot cylinder and he spun it as he walked to that cage. He pointed at gun towards the victim's head as he gave a grimaced smile to the man with the scars. He fired once, once more, a third time, a fourth time and on the fifth time he scowled with anger but in all instances, it was nothing but blank. Frustrated and perplexed as to why they bullet had not fired he pointed it to the ground, pulled the trigger and the bullet fired. What were the odds of that happening? This was the first time that no one had died playing this game.

At first the Gentleman was angry at his gun, but it wasn't long before he looked to the man with scars and smirked, "What rotten luck eh, looks like the sun is shining on you". He retired on that day and those souls were spared a horrible fate. On the second day the Gentleman changed the game, knowing the man with the scars would not exit his cage.

He waltzed passed the cages on that day and stopped

to talk to the man with the scars "My friend you see you are a bit of a spoiled sport. I really don't like spoilt sports. So, let's make this interesting". He gestured with one of his hand, out of the corner of the garden appeared a man with three ravenous dogs foaming at the mouth.

The Gentleman in an inquisitive tone said, "If you don't play my game well then I guess your fellow players can become dog meat". The dogs snarled and barked as those other men locked in their cages looked towards the man with the scars with fear racing in their eyes. The man looked back and hesitated for a while, eventually realising the situation he took a running position. The Gentleman looked to the man with the dogs and with his arms stretched out in a celebratory mood and a crooked smile he said, "I told you he would play". He looked at the man with the scars "Right now let me get into a position and eh wait for the siren". He took up his position, shortly after which the siren blared.

The man ran quicker than others that the Gentleman had seen before, he was quickly approaching the gate. The first shot that the Gentleman fired whistled passed the shoulder of the man. The second one flew over his head; he was almost at an arm's length from the gate when the third shot knocked him into a semi-conscious state. He remained their lying on the ground for a considerable time until he was lifted from the ground on a stretcher. In his lucid state he made out the Gentleman looking at him smiling, when he passed the cages, he saw the men he had tried to save being savagely mauled by those ravenous dogs.

This process was repeated over the period of one month till one eventful day. On that eventful day the process of this cruel torture was carried out like the many times he had been before. But this time the man with the scars was determined to escape. He ran faster than before and he reached the gate and even managed to touch it.

Only to be cut short by a bullet which hit him in the right leg crippling him. That was the day where the Gentleman abandoned him and forgot about him. These memories didn't really matter to him, there was no reason for him to dwell on the affairs of inferior people.

The Gentleman thoughts became preoccupied with preparation for an assault rather than his memories. There was no order as to who was going to be attacked next but in his gut the Gentleman knew it was him.

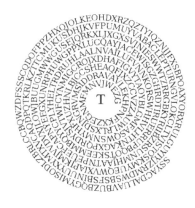

Chapter Twenty: One-man Army

If it wasn't obvious to the patriarchs in Europe already, they understood that the perpetrator who had committed these attacks was a single individual. He was more committed than an army and fearless in the face of such overwhelming odds.

Iron River had realised the effectiveness of this individual. How he had dispatched his enemies with such ease and disappeared with no trace, initially he had a thought of hiring him. Yet in the interest of his nation he wouldn't do it considering that this individual was after him. Trying to play this man to his advantage would inevitably lead to his death. So, being considerably smarter than the other patriarch's, he decided to understand the individual and wait patiently to seize a moment to spring a perfect trap. He looked at the remaining European patriarch's as perfect subjects and a buffer against any attack from the assailant.

The Mountain and the Gentleman both waited to see what would happen next. Several weeks had passed since Dark Star's death and nothing happened across Europe, or for that matter anywhere else in the world of note. This only made the Gentleman and the Mountain grow ever impatient and anxious. The Iron River had misgivings about trapping him now, given such a considerable time had passed, had he finally given up?

By now special agent Ramirez was slowly picking up the breadcrumbs which were left by the assailant. Through the careful examinations of whatever clues were present, there was still no clear understanding as to why the attacks really happened in New York or the attacks on the intelligence agencies of America.

Before Dark Star was killed, he planned to keep official government agents in the dark whilst redirecting them onto a different path. Ramirez was the only individual who knew something was up other than the ordinary. The official line from the government, which was carefully orchestrated by an unknown individual stated, 'the events which occurred in New York were a result of failed operation to capture members of a right-wing terrorist organisation'. Through his superiors that's what Ramirez had been told to investigate, 'A terrorist organisation with affiliations to the extreme right wing'.

Whilst that's what he did with the other agents officially, unofficially he decided to pursue his own line of investigation. The first breadcrumb Ramirez followed up on was a trace on the call he had received from Dark Star with the help of some good friends. This led him to a location which turned out to be in the middle of nowhere, clearly a means to make sure that Dark Star wasn't followed.

Even with this setback Ramirez persisted with his own investigation. He understood his and Dark Star's relationship was one that he had to be keep a secret. If any whisper of a relationship was passed to any of his superiors he would be compromised. There was a lot of so-called evidence which directed blame to this fantasy right-wing terrorist group, but he knew better. His persistence had led him to something which unbeknownst to Dark Star had slipped through his net of crafted lies.

Ramirez returned to the scene of the fire at the pier where he discovered a hard drive rather conveniently placed for him. His keen eyes had spotted it near an industrial trash can and from first glances it appeared as though it wasn't damaged. He retrieved it and began reviewing what was inside.

There were many files inside the hard drive but only one piqued Ramirez's interest a file marked 'watch me'. He opened the file and watched the video; he saw all the events that happened at the docks. He examined it frame by frame with a more perplexed face than before.

At first, he didn't understand as to what this video was truly showing. He had more questions than answers like who was this individual? Why was he doing this? But most importantly was someone helping him or misdirecting him?

Unbeknownst to Ramirez the assailant was slowly feeding him information coaxing him towards something for reasons unknown. How he had come to find Ramirez was equally puzzling. In the meanwhile, Ramirez remained cautious for he understood that he was treading down a treacherous path.

The information came through hard drives, letters and assortment of other means as Ramirez was beginning to slowly piece together as to what was going on? He knew now Dark Star was killed by the same individual that had killed those men near the Empire State building. He also knew that this individual was the one that had also committed the attacks on the intelligence agencies. Yet he still didn't understand as to why he was being given this evidence or by whom. Resolute, Ramirez had only objective to bring the assailant to justice and if this information could help, he would use it to his advantage.

A cold iron eye was watching, and the assailant had made his first fatal mistake. Iron River knew of Ramirez alongside everything that he was doing through his many eyes and ears. Which meant every piece of evidence which went through Ramirez's hands went through his. He knew there was an opening, a potential weakness to exploit, something he could use to his advantage to determine where this unexplained information was coming from.

There was however a lingering risk if he left the opportunity for too long then Ramirez would get what he wanted and expose everything. By killing him he too quickly he would lose his chance. So, he remained vigilant analysing Ramirez under a finer microscope but keeping a fair distance.

If it wasn't clear by now there was a single solitary man facing armies of men and winning. However now he was facing something which was lurking in the shadows, waiting for him to fall into a trap of convivence.

Chapter Twenty-One: Justice and Chaos

The careful balance of justice and chaos was a task that was difficult to maintain. The misgivings, the constant battle to argue whether what he was doing was right. Every man he had killed, every one of them who he had butchered were they deserving of his violence or were they just like him. These pesky gnawing thoughts chewed into the conscious of the assailant. At times when he would camp, he would stare into the abyss of the nights sky as these thoughts entered and left. Now however they were a tide raging against his thin wall which separated his ideals of chaos and justice.

Things were escalating beyond his control, now he had placed his trust in an individual he didn't really know. There was great a deal of conflict in the decision, to coax special agent Ramirez to make him understand as to why he was doing what he was doing. He knew as well as Ramirez that the evidence would indict him. He only took the decision, so he could confide in someone other than himself, yet the thought of Ramirez getting killed that was something that he could not let happen. Ramirez would either bring him to justice or he would learn and keep his secret until his dying old days.

Every time he reached these situations where his mind was constant state of flux, he took out that same rusted bronze locket. He opened and looked at the face within it and reminisced about home. The comfort and warmth of the dwindling fire, the sturdy chair which he used to sit in, the half-smoked pipe full of earthy leaves which lie to his left. The morning sun which slowly poured its way into the single pain windows lighting everything up. The boiling black cauldron filled with hearty stew; how could he forget that.

Last of all that unusual kindred laughter which came gleefully down the stairs with the smell of roses and exited in the early hours of morning through the front door. These reminiscent memories lingered after opening his locket they were a reality which could have been lived out to his very last day, but the assailant understood the task that he had undertaken. He knew it meant the distinct possibility that he would die with his sealed, dark and vicious memories rather than experience them once more.

For people such as the Gentleman they did not have notions of justice. In their minds, controlled chaos was something far more powerful. Yet soon enough he too would learn about justice as he waited mulling in fear, growing apprehensive as the days ticked by.

The Gentleman felt he had waited long enough now brewing in fear. Now it was his turn to rattle the feathers of the assailant. At first, he wondered how he would do that, but it wasn't long before he had an idea.

The attacks on the intelligence agencies of Russia,

France, USA, UK, Pakistan, India and China ruled out a secondary attack because of the increased security. Other than these attacks there had been the ambush at Bodie, Craco and New York which were all deliberate traps set up by the assailant. The Gentleman was aware that any clues or information as to the whereabouts of the assailant, gained by ease was more than certain a trap set up by the assailant. He was also aware a day attack was out of the ordinary for the assailant so an attack by night was more likely. From this knowledge he hatched his own ambush.

His idea, a particularly cruel one, was to advertise the of killing innocent people to play on the emotional strings of the assailant. For his plan to succeed he needed two things to happen. Number one was to find a way to get his attention. Number two, required him getting enough men in place to trap him. The second issue was no problem for him as he already had enough cronies working for him. The first issue however was going to be more difficult. After careful consideration calling upon his knowledge of human psychology he knew where he could place his message.

The Gentleman's strategy to the first issue was to deliberately place himself in a position which put him in direct danger. He would deliver speeches and interviews at security conferences and various new channels during daylight hours. Gradually increasing his reputation as an expert on all things security whilst simultaneously increasing the attention around him. While subtly mentioning under a guise of words in his speeches and interviews, his threat to kill innocent civilian unless the assailant showed himself at a certain place and time.

For weeks the Gentleman's had a gut feeling that he was next on the list of patriarchs to be attacked. The assailant had crossed out Dark Star's name on this list and the Gentleman was indeed next. The assailant was watching from a safe distance trying to understand the task he would face and the trap the Gentleman had set for him. Dark Star's mistake was to rely on his anger and sheer will to make his judgements. The Gentleman's mistake was his arrogance and false perceptions of safety.

The White Mountain was slightly wiser, he had seen first-hand the tactical brilliance and the combination of sheer violence. He knew that this precarious circumstance that he found himself meant he had to be cautious. The brazenness of the Gentleman was something that he would not follow suit in. It was in his opinion tactically stupid for he relied on his military experience to guide him.

He wasn't wrong to think this. There was nothing that could save the Gentleman from his prideful attitude now. The Mountain was content with leaving the Gentleman to his fate. All he would do was to watch, wait and prepare for the assault on him after the Gentleman was dead.

That indeed was the case because the assailant was in England scoping out the dread filled estate of the Gentleman eying up an assault.

Chapter Twenty-Two: Fire at the Estate

The Gentleman sat in a large chair with his tall, skinny and surprisingly strong body, it was lit up by the flickering flames from the roaring fire in the main royal living room. His eyes starred at the fire with confidence whilst his eyebrows faced downwards towards the bridge of his long and construed nose. His face was clean shaven, long and square. His slick oiled hair which ran from his right side to the left was without his familiar bowler hat. He smiled with his wry, crisp and sinister smile.

Today he was wearing his favourite tweed suit neatly sewn and ironed with a black tie. On his feet were black Oxford leather shoes instead of brown ones. They were pointed and shiny, crossed by his legs. He looked to his black Pinchbeck watch attached to his wrist, watching and waiting as the time ticked, smiling away with his infamous wry, crisp and sinister smile.

The antagonistic and confrontational approach by the Gentleman meant his face was on nearly every platform he could find. Even though he had arranged a place and time of his choosing, he still waited every night since Dark Star's death for an attack to come but now the time of his waiting was nearly over.

The last of the daylight was washed away by the ever the present and darkness and now it had turned into the evening. Slowly but surely the stars in the night sky were beginning to appear and inside the estate the Gentleman waited, now armed with a heavily modified Colt Walker in his left hand and a knife in the other as the set time grew nearer.

The grandfather clock in the central hallway ticked and tocked as the men walked the ground of the estate and on the roofs like the footmen of the queen's guard. The floorboards creaked with every passing of the footmen which walked upon it. The innocent people looked to the stars whilst their tears ran down their cheeks. The usual sounds of the house were the only things that could be heard with occasional crackle of radios waves, and the feint wailing of the people locked in the depths of the estate.

The sounds of the estate abruptly fell silent as the doorbell rang. The Gentleman's footmen ran to the door stopping with their guns fixed to it. One of them bravely opened it and there in the frame stood the man the Gentleman was after. The footmen barked at him to place his hands up, he complied and took three steps forward into the hallway of the estate as they took a step back. It wasn't long before the Gentleman came a little closer to see him. His face was giddy with joy at last he had done what the others couldn't. He had lured the very man who had alluded them for so long.

The Gentleman wasn't entirely consumed by his

joyous mood, he was aware that the man before him had escaped similar situations like this before. So, he kept his words short and sweet "I'm so happy you came… I enjoyed your little game but now I'm afraid it comes to an end". The assailant had entered almost accepting that he was going to die.

Before the assailant could do anything, the Gentleman raised his left hand and pointed the Colt at the assailant's head, with the full desire to kill this man that the other patriarchs couldn't. His aim was true, the bullet exited the chamber traveling a short distance in the air before it crunched into the mask of the assailant. The sound echoed in the estate as the assailant's head jerked back and his hands flailed forwards. His legs kicked forward as he fell backwards crashing into the ground. The back of his mask smacked against the marble floor rising from the impact before crashing down again.

His arms were slightly twisted, his legs straight and

his head facing to the side with what appeared to be blood seeping out from a cracked mask. It wasn't long before the Gentlemen made a remark in an enraptured mood, "I can't believe it was that easy! I should've taken my time…ah no matter all's well that ends well". He gestured to one of his footmen to look at the body just to make sure that the assailant was dead.

The footman walked over to check the body. He placed one hand on the barrel of his gun and the other on the neck of the assailant. There was no pulse, so he nodded his head right to left to right to indicate to the Gentleman that there was no life. The Gentleman acknowledged his gesture and then told him in an eager tone "Well go on the take of this idiot's mask let's see who we were fighting"? Both hands of the footman reached slowly for the mask. The Gentlemen and the rest of his men looked on in great anticipation. His hands got closer and closer and closer until the tips of his fingers were touching the mask.

Without Warning, the head of assailant suddenly swivelled around like a demonic spirit to come face to face with the footman. The assailant's left hand quickly wrapped around the footman's waist as it reached for his sidearm, whilst his right hand smashed into the footman's face leaving him dazed. The rest of the men looked visibly shocked as well as the Gentleman. The assailant took the side arm out of the holster and wrapped his legs around the footman rolling him over to the left side, as he quickly discharged shots into his stomach. He was right on top of the now deceased footman with his sidearm in his left hand. It wasn't long before the Gentlemen's men sporadically started firing into the back of the assailant. It did nothing to hinder or to slow the assailant down.

The shock of the Gentlemen turned into fear as he ran in the opposite direction towards the place where the hostages were being held. The assailant turned to face the nearest man on his left. He took two strides before leaping forward into the air with his gun pointing forward. He discharged two shots killing the man whilst the forward moving mass of the assailant knocked his victim further way.

The assailant threw the now empty gun to the man nearest to the door staggering him before dropping a blue knife from his arm and charging at him, quickly severing his arteries at the neck. The rest of the men took cover behind whatever they could find increasing their fire. The assailant expertly jumped, dived and rolled to different points before dispatching each man. It wasn't long before he had killed every man in the hallway.

He removed the broken mask on his face to reveal the real one underneath. He made his way down the hallway towards the hostages as more men from the estate gardens and the roof poured into the house. They fired upon him whilst he ran deeper into the estate.

He made sure to bar each door which he raced past and placed a device on the last one. Soon he reached the room where the Gentleman was face to face with him. He stood there with four men on a raised platform with their guns trained on at least thirty people. The Gentlemen made it apparent as to what would happen if the assailant made one false move, "It seems you're in a pickle here".

He took a short breath before speaking again with his gun pointed at the assailant, "You are playing my game now; you move they die you got that".

The sound of gunfire was getting closer as the Gentleman's men broke down each door which had been barred by the assailant. The Gentleman looked at the assailant shaking his head in disbelief and in anger, "How are you not dead? This is isn't very sportsmanlike of you is it"? The assailant didn't respond.

The Gentleman reassured by the sounds of his men getting closer decided to stall, "You don't like to talk, do you? No matter it will be over soon".

He brandished his gun a little more intently and haphazardly, "You're playing my game now, let's start off with something simple. Take of your armour and place that knife on the floor slowly".

The assailant didn't comply, so the Gentlemen raised his voice whilst in the background the sound of the Gentleman's men grew louder, "I said take of your armour and place the knife on the floor slowly"!

Again, the assailant didn't comply which lead to the gentlemen threatening the hostages and raised his voice even more, "If you don't comply you know what's going to happen"!

The mask on the head of the assailant turned into a red led emoji with a sinister smile. As this happened the floor collapsed beneath the hostages. The Gentlemen looked on in horror almost gawking to see the assailant leaping towards him. The four men beside him were quickly dispatched he on the other hand was severely wounded but not dead.

It was about then the doors to the room the assailant was in burst open, only to be blown apart by the device attached to it. The shards of timber and explosion ripped into the men entering canvassing the bare walls with their flesh and blood. Whoever remained was picked of in the night. The hostages who were unconscious were freed by the assailant, and he made sure to return each one to their homes.

As for the Gentleman he was dragged into the office unconscious from the blood loss from his wound. When he awoke, he was soaked in fuel. He saw the assailant dousing his office in fuel and around him was all his men. The Gentleman looked to him and begged for mercy the assailant took no pity. From one of his pockets he produced an incendiary flare. He popped it off and threw it on to the Gentleman, he screamed as it slowly burned him. He tried to move and when he did bits of his

precious of estate rapidly caught fire. After a few minutes

the whole estate was on fire and bits of the roof crumbled

inwards as the walls collapsed. The assailant watched

from afar as the blaze lit up the night sky.

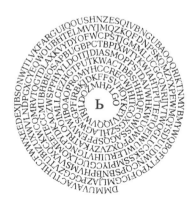

Chapter Twenty-Three: The Hanged Man

It wasn't long before the news of the Gentleman had reached the ears of the White Mountain. He knew it was only going to be a matter days before the assailant would be at his door looking for his next scalp. Iron River on the other hand was more focused on acquiring more information about the assailant, at the expense of his colleague's death. He had learned from Dark Star's death the trickery of the assailant. From the death of the Gentleman he had learned the boldness of the assailant. But most importantly of all he had learned of his unwillingness to die until every one of the patriarchs was dead.

For the White Mountain his death was about to be made certain. The Mountain was an old soldier that had done his fair share of dirty work for his nation. He had killed many of France's enemies, in his eyes they were all justified by his government. Through his experiences in conflict he had grown to the rank of major and earned many prestigious medals. Yet in his heart he was discontent with his superiors for failing to uphold his notions of French ideals and culture.

He felt betrayed at times with his government, for choosing peace over war. He had archaic ideas about as to where France should be heading. His service for his country as a soldier and the people he had killed and the medals that he had won didn't matter to him. For behind this man filled with distinguished service to his country, was a man who was divested in methods which were neither legal nor humane.

After his days as a soldier he joined the intelligence services of France. At first, he took small cases which gradually grew bigger and bigger till eventually he had risen through the ranks. For each step he took up this ladder, he took two steps into an abyss of torture.

The first day he took to these methods was the day everything changed. It was the eighth of May on World War two victory day he hadn't taken the day off. The Mountain wasn't feeling too victorious that day he was irritated by the lack of progress he was making on a case. The suspects in that case were innocent but he judged them to be guilty, yet he couldn't prove it. He was sitting in the office on the phone arguing for a warrant to be given from his superior. On every occasion he asked, he was declined due to lack of evidence.

He sat there contemplating a way forward that was until he picked up a book which he found lying about. It wasn't long before he was invested into it, the book detailed France's history from the past to the present day. There was a singular part of the book which detailed the extraordinary violence which occurred during the French revolution. He became transfixed with the idea of hanging and for days after reading the book he thought about it, maybe because of his own dissociation from French society.

It wasn't long before he gave into his worst inhibitions, the notion of killing was to him a mundane task and that of torture, well that was nothing. At first, he used the hangings as a mean of torture to get the false evidence he desired. On occasion he would sometimes hang a man without extracting any evidence at all even if he was innocent of the accused crime.

It wasn't long after that before it became more a tool for a sadist rather a means of acquiring information. Over time his methods had developed, and he was doing more than just hanging men. The bodies began to rack up, the dead people had it easy, the people who he didn't kill they had it much worse.

In a hollowed-out shell of a cell he had any number of people in various stays of decay and despair. The nature of what he was had changed completely. In that cell he would take any person that he assumed to be guilty, then he strapped them to those archaic stretching racks. He would begin by asking simple questions if they didn't listen, he would begin to turn the wheel pulling their arms and legs. He did this to make sure they confessed to crimes they had not committed. The pain he plied would gradually coax the victim into confessing in order to stop the torture.

Sometimes he would meet souls who were just willing to die for what they had gone through was enough. He would never grant their wish but always flirt with the possibility of doing it. The victims were sometimes strung up by a hangman's knot delicately balancing on a four-legged stool. For a few moments he would stare at his victims' eyes almost sucking their emotions from their weakened hearts. This would continue for a while until the victims would beg him to end it. If it ever did happen, the Mountain would raise a pistol shooting each leg one by one till the victims slowly struggled. On most occasions the Mountain made sure to cut the knot before they were suffocated to death.

The last method he had was considerably crueller than the rest. The people he hated the most were Arabs, Blacks, Socialists, Liberals, Conservatives and most of all Republicans. If anyone of these individuals was even a suspected of a crime, he used this last from of torture.

The torture involved strong metal wire which was attached to a motor. The process involved the victim being strapped down to the same stretching rack but this time a steel wire was placed around the waist of the victim. Then the mountain would ply the pain, for the victims there was no survival, so it really didn't matter how they answered. Eventually towards end, the wire would tighten so much it would rip the body of the victim cleanly in half. They would always remain conscious for a while screaming and writhing in anguish until blood would spew out form their mouth and their souls would rescind into nothingness.

There was a day where he was brought individual who had been suspected of stealing. This individual received such an experience that it could not compare to what he had done to his other victims. It began all the same, first the Mountain would starve his victims. He would provide just the right amount of water and food that kept them alive. Then he subjugated them to a sound of his preference, repeatedly. Usually this went on for a month then he would begin the physical torture. However, the man who had been accused of stealing endured that month with ease. He didn't appear to be hungry or broken psychologically.

Impressed by his endurance, he extended the period of degradation by another month. When that passed, he once again extended it and two more after that. After five months of this degradation the Mountain relented and then began a whole month of torture. The intent of the mountain was to kill eventually, but for his own satisfaction he toyed with him.

He plied his forms of torture hour after hour, day after day and week upon week. The victim never talked although he occasionally grunted in pain. Eventually the Mountain began to admire the resilience of this victim and took a liking to him. That was until one day the Mountain entered the cell in an unbridled rage and decided to kill him.

This man who had endured six months of degradation and torture was strung by his neck on the stool with four legs. The mountain blew away the first three legs as the man precariously balanced himself on the last leg. On the last leg the Mountain hesitated it wasn't because he was struck by empathy, but it was something else entirely. The man was staring at him with great, flaming eyes of anger. He held his gaze at the Mountain for at least minute. The Mountain stared right back at him for the same amount of time until the man eventually blinked. Then the final shot went off and the last leg shattered. To the Mountain's surprise the hanging wasn't instant. The man resisted and fought for a considerable time. Upon witnessing this the Mountain shot the rope and the man fell to the floor.

The man was unfazed, and his eyes were still burning with rage, it made the Mountain feel uncomfortable. After that he never tortured him again and eventually, he moved him elsewhere.

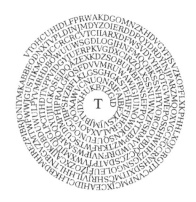

Chapter Twenty-Four: Relief

Relief was there any? Did they know of any? Did they give any? No mercy was ever evident in all these deaths and there wasn't going to be any relief. Now there was an uncontrollable tide which was raging against pain, injustice and despair.

At the ambush at Bodie SGT. Riley asked for relief in the form of mercy. In Craco the Mountain had assumed his men were safe in their sanctity of relief. At the estate the Gentleman found relief in the assailant's capture. When they were in their palaces made of gold and thrones of blood and bones and with their armies at their command, they had relief. They were living in bliss unaware of the danger lurking in the shadows. The assailant showed no mercy, he had shown no regard for his own safety and no regard for petty victories. Dark Star was dead, the Gentleman was dead, the Mountain and Iron River were next. Their crimes would not go unpunished they would suffer and die.

The Mountain assumed he was wiser than his counterparts which were dead. His mistake was to play the experience card. His understanding was simplistic and ignorant. He had miss-assumed that the assailant was a man of no experience. He thought his military views would be enough to overcome this challenge.

Iron River understood the more significant intellectual capacity of the Mountain, so he decided to assist, albeit for his own deceptive intentions. The relief which Iron River provided the Mountain was also a contentious issue. Iron River himself was not present in Paris but he assisted the Frenchmen with much needed men. They were not ordinary ones too, these men were highly trained, effective in close quarter combat and all former soldiers from the Spetnasz.

The Mountain was a very detailed man, from his

militaristic nature he drew up his plan of action. His plan was to stand his ground, he knew from his previous attempts that an overwhelming force of men and firepower would play to the assailant's advantage. The specialized men provided by Iron River would certainly give him the edge over the assailant.

He unlike the Gentlemen and Dark Star also considered as to where he might position himself if he had to fight. The Mountain understood the layout of Paris well, this would play to his advantage. There were several other things he also considered the weather and the time. Previously he had been outwitted by the assailant when the fog rolled in over the ruins of Craco as a result he lost one of his best sub lieutenants. The last issue was that of discretion, he didn't want any more eyes on these events.

If the assailant was to come for him, he would lure him somewhere which was favourable for him. The confines of the city streets and the catacombs would play to the assailant's advantage. Therefore, he decided that if the assailant attacked, he would retreat to the forest of Saint Germain en laye. His men would entrench themselves in pre fortified areas and wait for him to attack. This time he wouldn't retreat like he did in Craco. That was the plan, but nothing ever goes to plan there are always hiccups and factors which you can't consider. One such factor is knowing how your enemy will react.

The man who was coming to kill the Mountain had crossed the channel and was in France. More importantly he was in Paris and he was preparing to kill the Mountain, formulating plans of his own in order to so. The Mountain had discussed his plans with Iron River, he outwardly expressed to the Mountain that it was fine. However inwardly he knew it was going to fail. The men he had placed were only there on his commands to observe and should things turn South they were to not engage.

In the meantime, the Mountain was cooped up in a chateau deep in Paris which was heavily guarded with his own men, patrolling the area like clockwork. There was a dilemma the Mountain faced with his plan, how was he to make sure the assailant was to follow him? His intuitions alone were not going to cut it, the Gentleman had attempted to lure the assailant with hostages he failed. Dark star took the initiative to the assailant and he also failed.

For the assailant to follow the Mountain into the park the Mountain decided to lower the security surrounding him if things went awry. He hoped by doing this the assailant would be incentivised by the drive to kill the him and the easy possibility of doing so.

The Mountain felt confident in his ability. His assumptions led him to believe the weaker he appeared the stronger position he was in. There were two things which had left the mountain in a favourable position. The assailant did not know of the extra men Iron River had sent and the final place in which the Mountain was going to attempt to kill the assailant. The Mountain was already dreaming about his plan succeeding and him finally being able to rest with no vengeful eyes watching his back.

Chapter Twenty-Five: Mutiny at the Forest

It was the early hours of the morning In Paris, the Mountain was enjoying his morning coffee in his office. The room was dimly lit by the fire in his fireplace. There was very few Parisian's on the streets as it was the early morning and the nearby roads had been closed for maintenance. The Mountain's men were doing there morning rounds walking up and down his chateau.

It was like this for a while, until through the corner of the Mountain's eye he saw one of his men fall into the courtyard. He jumped to his feet running quickly to get his gun. The windowpanes in his office shattered as bullets pierced them and made large cavernous holes in the walls of his office. The Mountain managed to get his gun and made a dash for the door as a bullet skimmed passed by him. He ran down the stairs heading towards his car as his men rushed to him. Bodies fell from the tops of the roof of the chateau, one of which fell directly on the car of the Mountain causing his screen to shatter and blood to be spattered over it. His men quickly bungled him into the car and reversed dropping the body on to the courtyard. The car drove out and on to the open streets as bullets pinged of the back of it.

The assailant who was firing from the rooftops seized fire as soon as he saw the Mountain's car leave the courtyard. It wasn't long before he was chasing the Mountain by jumping, running and rolling unto the Parisian rooftops and roads. The car was considerably quicker than the assailant, but he managed to predict its path.

The car rapidly raced away from the assailant vanishing into the streets. Fortunately for the assailant he had managed to fire a tracer on the car before the Mountain had sped off. He continued his pursuit and eventually he arrived at the destination to where the car was. He waited for a short while to catch his breath in a ditch on the side of a road, before he released a tirade of bullets at the vehicle. When he finished, he walked over to the car only to find the Mountain was not there. The realisation hit him; he had fallen into a trap.

The Mountain's men were patiently waiting, well hidden in the trenches that they had pre-dug in the Saint-Germain-en-lay forest. They were stationed in a circle around the car, not too far from the assailant. Some of the men with the Mountain were Russians who were stationed in the North of the tree line, South of the Seine. Although Iron River had given the permission for the Mountain to give orders to his men, they were secretly told by him not to obey.

The assailant for the first time felt disorientated not knowing from which way the attack was going to come from. It wasn't long before sporadic fire broke out, bullets whistled past the trees hitting his armour as men from all angles descended on him. The shock from the heavy bullets quickly winded him as the men came closer and closer. The assailant crawled towards the underside of the car whilst bullets pinged of the car.

Soon they were just a few meters away from him. The bullets from the encroaching fire shattered the glass on the car as others punctured holes into the car exterior. The initial shock from the impact of the bullets became subdued and the assailant was back to thinking on his feet again. He reached down his right leg and pulled out his holstered pistol. He rolled onto his right side and out under the car. By using the car as cover for his back his kneeled on one knee and fired back on the oncoming wave of men and the entrenched positions. He deployed a shield enclosed in a case on his left arm blocking most of the frontal fire. In quick succession the men in front of him were dropping like flies. Some of them decided to take cover but to no avail and very quickly the frontal wave was down.

The rear attack and flanking attacks tried to rush the assailant. He was quick to react and ran toward the oncoming men. He shot the first man clean though the head whilst sliding under him and spin kicking the next, shooting down all the remaining men on his rear. He quickly turned to his extendable sword cutting down all on those entrenched to the right and left of him. Using his pistol, sword and shield it was quickly demonstrated that the assailant had no match in close quarter combat.

In the space of five minutes the assailant had effectively wiped half of the Mountain's fighting force. The Mountain was unrelenting opting for a second wave of attack, though this time he took the forest as an advantage deciding to remain entrenched. Some of the men confused by the disorienting array of trees, quick movements of the assailants and coupled with the screams of dying men cowardly abandoned their posts.

The Mountain displeased with them executed at least ten of his own men as they ran out from the treeline. The remnants of the Mountain's force which was entrenched below the trees was quickly wiped out, in a last ditch attempt he called upon the remaining Russians to attack the assailant. His call was met with silence, he tried again and again but it was met by silence. The Russians had observed what they wanted to and were escaping on boats down the Siene. All hope was lost now for support. The Mountain who was standing alone watched the Russians flee. His plan was in shreds now his mind was awash with anger.

A figure came through the treeline bloodied as he pleaded for help. Behind him the assailant, who drove his blade through the figure and dropped him to the side like a dead piece of meat. The attention of the Mountain was on the assailant who was dripping in blood. The assailant looked at him and wiped his hand against his coat.

For a while they stared at each other until the Mountain charged towards the assailant firing the gun in his white knuckled hands. The bullets pinged of the assailant who remained still as he came closer and closer. The assailant looked on, exhausted but determined. When the Mountain was within an arm's length of the assailant, he smashed his shield into him knocking him to the ground. The Mountain shuddered in pain unable to move. The assailant reached into one of his trench coat pockets and pulled out a wire he went over to the Mountain and wrapped it around his neck. The Mountain resisted and fought hard to breath but soon the glimmer of life within his eyes faded and the Mountain succumbed to his death.

The assailant left the lifeless corpse of the Mountain in the field. He looked at the injuries he had sustained and realised how close he had come to failure. He trudged away making sure that he left no trace of his existence.

Chapter Twenty-Six: Revelations

It wasn't long before the news of the Mountain and his men's death had spread. Every major news organisation in France and in the world was reporting on it. They assumed that the killings were a result of gang violence; the government also corroborated these notions per the well-executed contingency plan of the Mountain.

The news had reached Ramirez who upon hearing it decided to go to France to investigate these reports. He made the necessary arrangements and made his way there. Albeit he did not have permission from his superiors or even a warrant. He covered himself by claiming that he was going on holiday much to the surprise of his fellow colleagues who were investigating the attack at New York. Ramirez understood it wouldn't be long before they got suspicious if he overextended his stay in Paris, so he decided to keep it short and not mention as to where he was going. Upon arriving he decided to stay in a nearby hotel due to its proximity to the location. To get close to the scene he knew that he would have to make up some excuses, but for now that could wait first, he was going to rest.

In the morning when he awoke and got ready to travel to the place where the Mountain had died, positioned under the door he found a strange unmarked letter. Upon opening it he found a flash drive he examined it for a while before placing it in his personal laptop. He moved his cursor into the computer file and clicked on the flash drive named 'spindle'. In that flash drive was a one file addressed 'friend'. At first Ramirez was cautious as to open it. He thought about it and considered whether it might from the same individual who had been giving him information from the incident in New York.

Eventually he gave into curiosity and opened the file, inside the file was a video which he examined carefully going through each frame. In the video he saw a man who appeared very familiar to him and a second man not so familiar. He sat watching it repeatedly until he realised who one of the men was, it was Dark Star and he was talking to him. This video if anything was a threat made personally to him. Ramirez may have been slightly disturbed by the video but was still undeterred.

He should not have followed the breadcrumbs as there were foreboding signs across in the sky. There were eyes watching him ones that he could not have known about. They were the eyes of Iron River who through the eyes of others, was aware of what information Ramirez had stumbled upon. A degree of threat was still posed by Ramirez, if he was to ever find out the things that he or Dark Star did, it would be the end of him.

Upon finishing watching the video Ramirez made his way down to the crime scene. There was a significant police and press presence and there was no easy way around it. Ramirez tried to persuade the policemen to let him pass but to no avail. He looked around for an opening to slip past the police and investigators. Eventually he found one, it was to the side of the road through the forest, he slipped passed the guards and was careful to properly conceal himself against the trees. He made his way to the crime scene and observed the forensic investigators and police officers, scouring the scene for at least twenty minutes. It wasn't long before something caught his eye, it was a young girl moving around near the press pool. She was small and skinny in appearance and she seemed to be watching the crime scene rather intently. At first Ramirez thought to forget about it but for some unconscious reason he decided to find out who she was.

He slipped out of the forest and back into the press pool making his way towards the girl. The girl noticed him and quickly started to walk away from Ramirez. He followed her down the road as she slowly picked up her pace and eventually started running as Ramirez followed. The girl eventually stopped in a side road to look and saw that no one was behind her. She put her hands on her knees and panted for air, making her way to her apartment. She looked down the street one last time to check if someone had followed and no one had. Ramirez had fallen back on purpose as he knew he would not be able to catch her, as she would have easily evaded him in all the unfamiliar side streets. So, he decided to track her down using other means.

He retired back to his hotel room and began to investigate as to where this girl lived. Luckily for Ramirez there were several shops in the area where he saw the girl run past, some of these shops had CCTV cameras. The issue of getting the shopkeepers to show him the footage was going to be difficult. Instead of asking the shopkeepers he decided to sneak in, somehow, he manged to do this a couple of times. In all other instances he manged to persuade the shopkeepers to review their CCTV footage. It wasn't long before he had worked out where she lived. The building where she lived was a block of flats it was next to a football field and the address was fifty-three Avenue du Parc, 95100 Argenteuil.

It took Ramirez a few days to discover this information, yet there was no certainty of her being there. He had managed to acquire a photograph of the girl from the CCTV printed from a local printer in a computer shop. It was a great tool, but it didn't help that he didn't know French, but most of the locals understood what he as asking for.

He went through the front door of the apartment block and up the stairs and made his way to the apartment. Before long he was near a dilapidated black door with some of the paint peeling away from it.

Ramirez knocked on the door, the sound of locks opening was the first thing that he heard. The door opened revealing a shy and reclusive girl, she looked down at the feet of Ramirez slowly raising her head to look up towards the face Ramirez. At first, she froze not knowing who the face of the man that she was looking at. She quickly snapped out of the momentary lapse in concentration and tried to slam the door shut.

The door however did not close, Ramirez had placed his left foot between the door and the frame preventing her from closing it. Realising that she could not close the door she staggered backwards, frantically searching left and right across the room for anything that she could use to defend herself. Ramirez entered the room with a reassuring face as he gestured with his hands that he meant no harm. The girl stumbled into the kitchen and reached into the utensil drawer where she found a knife. Ramirez got closer trying to ease the girl. The girl in

French made it clear that she would swing if he came any closer.

Realising that this was going nowhere he took a few paces back, as she trembled brandishing the knife. He reached into his pocket and slowly pulled out a picture of her. He asked her "This is you isn't it"? She looked at the picture trembling in fear and nodded her head.

Ramirez pressed on with a second question with a slow monosyllabic tone, "I need your help; I know you saw something? I just want to know what was it that you saw"?

The girl hesitated before softly replying in a broken English accent "Ok, but first tell me who you are"?

Ramirez reached once more into his pocket and the girl quickly stiffened her grip on the knife making sure it was pointed at Ramirez. He pulled out his badge "I am an agent who works for the FBI if you want you can look at my badge".

She signalled for him to throw it on the floor towards her. She picked it up and examined the contents for a while before loosening her stance with her knife. Satisfied she threw the badge back towards him, before letting of a huge sigh of relief. Ramirez sat down on the couch on his side and told her that he would not be long. She looked at him rather begrudgingly realising that Ramirez would not stop till he got some answers.

She put away the knife and sat down to talk to him. The conversation went on for about an hour, until Ramirez was satisfied with the information he had received. He thanked her and told her not to tell anyone that he had come here. He made reassurances to her that he would not dispel anything that she had told him. Eventually he left the apartment complex and made his way to central Paris.

Chapter Twenty-Seven: Asian Patriarchs

The assailant had killed Dark Star, the Gentlemen, and the Mountain all because of a singular weakness which he had exploited. Dark Star had died because he failed to control his hate and aggression, the Gentlemen died because of his naivety and the mountain his reliance on outdated experience and failing to seize the moment. The group he had neglected was the Asian patriarchs. They had each suffered a devastating attack on their bases, but no secondary attacks had followed.

It wasn't through choice that the assailant had neglected them but because there were undeniable reasons which prevented him. The assailant understood the distance he would have to travel, the necessary arrangements he would have to make, the effort would be immeasurable. That was just the logistics of the whole operation, it would have been nearly made almost possible, for these patriarchs were notoriously difficult to find. Yet the real reason as to why the assailant had neglected them was because he was unsure whether he would make it past the Iron River. If he could just get over this last hurdle maybe he would be able to finish of the rest.

These remaining patriarchs unlike the other patriarchs did not share links with one another as neither knew of the other. The only connection they had was with the Iron River who knew all of them. The Iron River had realised the benefits from these nations, choosing to prevent conflict with them in order to strengthen his own nations standing.

Unlike that of the Europeans who had existing links since the formation of NATO. It wasn't until the collapse of the Soviet Union did the Iron River join this small gathering of sorts pretending to be non-belligerent. In truth however, he had always tried to play the situation to his advantage, but he could never get around any of them, they were always there to hinder him. But now the game had changed they were all dead and there was no obstacle in his way expect that of the assailant whom he was marginally closer to capturing.

All the patriarchs had their individual quirks and uniqueness which defined them for who they were, that was also true of the Asian patriarchs. There had always existed three but unlike the others there was a woman amongst their ranks. The woman's name was Jade Dragon, a name which was often attached with something grand in stature. Yet the name of this woman was deceiving and purposely so.

Face to face her appearance was of an old, wrinkled and stumpy, woman. Her hair was wispy thin and white, it was fixed tight into a bun with a small black clip in the shape of a Chinese dragon. Her clothing was a black tangzhuang jacket embroided with two black dragons tinted with a sliver of jade on either side of the jacket. She wore a short white shirt underneath it with plain black trousers.

If you saw her right hand, you would see that she had five gold rings on each finger. It is said it is of her five husbands whom she had once been married to and had killed. She came from the coastal city of canton born to a poor spear fisherman; her mother died when she was young as did her father. For much of her life she was raised by her aunts and uncles, and always claimed affinity to the famous female pirate Shi Yang.

For much of her life she served as a worker for the Communist of party of China and remained passionately Communist, slowly working her way up the ranks. She was synonymous for her actions in the Sino-Vietnamese war, from which later she became an integral member of the Air intelligence division. Old age and attitudes of senior members forced her to retire.

As of late she ran a fisheries business and often could be seen with two hands behind her back trudging along. Often with two guards flanking her sides. But that's what everyone else saw, secretly she dabbled in all things nefarious. In the bowels of her factories there were tales of what she would do to those people who had crossed her. Those tales can't be corroborated due to the fact many of the tale tellers are all dead.

One other such individual that made the Asian patriarchs was a man who went by the name Broken Crescent. He was not to well known amongst his own ranks but if you ever came across him you would notice things that just didn't seem right. He had his eyes fixed into stare which were always looking into an abyss, it seemed like he never blinked. His hair was always slicked back, and it was dark brown in colour with small streaks of grey. His skin was considerably light and still young but the small white flickers of silvery white hair in his stubble gave away his age.

He wore a traditional salwar kameez in either white, black or a tweedish brown. He adorned a Peshawari style hat with the insignia of a major emblazoned across it. Often, he wore these funny rough black leather boots even in the scorching sun. To complete his look, he wore a military style jacket on top. One thing could always be said of his clothes they were always crisp, clean and free of creases.

From afar he looked tall and strong upon closer inspection it was nothing but the eyes that made him appear both intimidating and taller. The fairness of his skin and build was due to his parents who both hailed from the region known as KPK.

His father had imprinted within him the structure of being a soldier as his father was a soldier before him. Yet somehow none of that really sank in, in truth it was his bad behaviour that had ended him up in military college which turned him into a soldier. From there he served in a few conflicts in which he lost several his comrades which greatly affected his psyche. He retired with the rank of major from the army. Soon after he began a so-called low order operational command in the ISI. It was nothing but a cover for the actions he committed against the wishes of his government.

His personality was one of the most perplexing, although there may have been some degree of military doctrine instilled within him it seemed this had little effect on how he operated. His attitude was gun ho, with no real retrospective plan in mind. His actions were almost always insane, he was lucky that no one had stopped him yet because of his sloppy work. His unhinged psyche and the fact that he used the cover of the moon gave birth the name Broken Crescent amongst some other far nefarious reasons.

The last member of the individuals known as the

Asian patriarchs was the Frozen Claw. In appearance his build was like the Broken Crescent with a few notable exceptions to this. The stature of the Frozen Claw was taller, the skin on his face was darker and the middle of his head was balding. His hair had grown entirely white and wispy thin nonetheless it was neat and tidy. The eyes were sinister, black and brown in colour whilst his face almost clean shaven with the notable exception of his great, big, bushy moustache.

The attire was not too dissimilar to that of the Broken crescent, but his clothing was always white. On top of his salwar kameez he adorned a short black sherwani with black buttons and a singular black pocket on his top left-hand side, within it one solitary gold pen. To cover his balding hair, he would place on a Gandhi cap which in small letters had the letters MG stitched into it. On his left hand was a string bracelet and old brass timepiece. Due to old age it was not uncommon to see him dawdling along with a maple walking stick.

Of his origins there was never much, apart from being born in Uttar Pradesh and into to a large family. He had shown a desire to correct injustices by stamping out the unjust, what that exactly meant was anyone's guess.

He had known affiliations to the Indian army because of his service in many of the wars with Pakistan. He held the rank of corporal slowly progressing through the ranks and eventually becoming Major General. He retired from active service in the infantry and moved over to the Military police. It was there where he served as a high-ranking service for several years before adopting an advisory role to officials in India's RAW. It was anything short of advisory in nature, amongst his many victims were Sikh separatists, Communists and Kashmiris.

His unnatural desire and tolerance for the bitter Himalayan cold was often present in the way he would treat his victims. He was always, cool, calm and collected choosing to delay his fury until it suddenly fell upon his victims with tremendous force.

These patriarchs were just as vicious and evil as the others, for now they had been spared. Their time of reckoning would come with all its ruthless power.

Chapter Twenty-Eight: Wounded

The assailant had been wounded quite badly after his fight against the Mountain. His armour was only so good against successive near range gunshots, most of which had shattered or crumpled on him or his surroundings causing significant damage via shrapnel. The assailant was prepared for an eventuality such as this, he had placed a small bag containing all the vital things that he might need after sustaining damages such as this.

After the fight against the Mountain he had retreated far to a small ski chalet which he had rented out under an alias. It was east of Paris, not that far from the city of Strasbourg. The assailant understood that whatever was in the bag was a way away, so he had to make do with whatever he could find along the way. He looted small pharmacies along the way with as much discretion that he could. When he did reach the chalet, he dressed his wounds and found whatever sleep he could. The wounds however were stopping him from doing so.

He had a severe laceration on his left arm from which he brandished his shield, it was ballooning constantly with pain in a rhythmic motion. His right hand was partially fractured in several places and there was bruising and cuts all over his body. He was in no state to fight let alone walk. He had rented out the chalet for a week, but it was not enough time to recover from his wounds. Yet the looming possibility of being caught was something that he had to consider; he was a sitting duck on the top of a mountain.

On his fifth day of stay at the chalet he decided to move on into the city of Strasbourg and find a more welcoming abode. He used another alias and entered a small rundown block of apartments. He paid the landlord what he was due and made the plan to stay there for at least a month. That was easier said than done now he was at his most vulnerable and he was falling prey to hallucinogenic thoughts which were plaguing his mind.

The plan had been to kill the Mountain and move on, but the firefight had been more intense than he could have imagined. Worse still than the wounds he had sustained was the thought that the position of Iron River had been strengthened. It was almost like leaving a gaping wound open and allowing the most harmful of parasites to enter and slowly gnaw at the flesh.

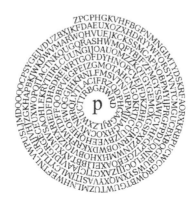

Chapter Twenty-Nine: The Bear's Claws

Ramirez who had now had an unjustifiable holiday was running out of excuses, he had to get back to work. The anticipation of finally nailing this mysterious individual was however far more compelling. The girl that he had interrogated had proven useful after following up on some unseen footage from the girl, had now been able to trace the assailant to the ski chalet near Strasbourg. It wasn't long before he discovered that he had used an alias and paid in cash to owner of the chalet. Yet there was a problem the owner had no idea where he went, Ramirez had struck a dead end.

After a few hours pondering in a local bar, he tried his luck in Strasbourg as it was the largest city nearest to the Chalet. The assailant had been diligent to remove any equipment that he used in the chalet or any trace that he was there except for the signature. Nonetheless Ramirez knew he was wounded from viewing the video, so he knew he would not go too far to recover.

But just where in Strasbourg was, he? He spent another day searching and examining the routes he could have taken and the places he could have stayed, up until the point he found the place. It was lucky really there was no deductive reasoning just sheer dumb luck. He was walking through some alleyway whereupon he stumbled upon the conversations of two French men. His French was far from perfect, but Ramirez was able to realise what the two men were talking about based on their gestures and attitude. One of the men was in a joyous flashing a bundle of cash to his friend, explaining how a man had overpaid him to stay in his apartment. He commented on the fact that he looked pretty bunged up.

Ramirez was sure that this man was talking about the person he was looking for. He just had to now work out which floor and which apartment. Through some easy enquiries he found out the apartment he was interested in. The apartment was number four hundred and four, on the third floor. He decided not to wait and made his way quickly into the building.

Although Ramirez was armed, he was uncertain as to what was behind the door. When he reached the floor upon which the apartment was located, he slowed down and drew his pistol and traversed slowly, careful not make any noise. The small narrow hallway upon which the doors of other apartments were located was quiet. Slowly but surely Ramirez made his way to the door, he was standing just to the left of the door and was considering his options. At first, he thought about shooting the lock off and breaking the door down but realised that would cause to much noise. He then considered to pose as a concerned neighbour, but his French was non-existent. The last idea was probably the worst one climb in from the window around the back of the apartment, which was nearly fifteen meters from the ground.

His mind tried to work out which was best, eventually he decided to opt for something a little subtler, a knock on the door. There was no way that the assailant would know it was him as there were no cameras and no door viewer. He was hoping to break and barge in and knock the assailant to the ground. The problem was this was the first time he had done anything like this on his own without back up.

His palms were sweating and the grip on his gun was slowly loosening. He found the courage to knock on the door. His hand reached out trembling slightly in fear and knocked three times hard and fast. He quickly withdrew his hand and reaffirmed his grip on his gun. He heard footsteps approaching the door and readied himself. The sound of the locks opening raised his heart rate further, then the door slowly opened, he waited until there was enough room to make his move. When the door had opened three quarters of the way Ramirez mustered his courage, gritted his teeth and surged forward.

Courage soon turned to fear, he had only made it a footstep in and was quickly struck on back of the head and fell to the floor. The gun fumbled away from him, as he struggled to compose himself. His mind was in a swirling descent of confusion mixed with adrenaline and fear. He tried to make out his surroundings as the shock of the first strike was quickly followed up by the second blow. That's when the hazy cloud of confusion went dark, Ramirez was out cold on the floor.

The eyes of Ramirez flickered opened, as his head tried to make sense of his surroundings. The smouldering pain of the blow which had struck him now began to bloom. When the colour and sense of depth returned to his eyes and body, it was met with the figure of the assailant. The whites in the eyes of Ramirez ballooned.

He tried to rise from the dilapidated armchair upon which he was sat on and run but the assailant simply gestured at his gun and he sat back down again.

Ramirez realised he had nowhere to run, yet it was puzzled as to why he wasn't dead already. He tried to conjugate something to say but he couldn't think of what. He was just fixed with appearance of the assailant sitting calmly in another armchair opposite to him with a gun in his hand. Ramirez looked around again to formulate a plan of escape but saw that the door and window were both sealed.

The assailant clicked his fingers to draw the attention of Ramirez, he promptly turned his attention to him. The assailant reached into his pocket and pulled out a hardrive and threw it to Ramirez. He then gestured to Ramirez to plug it into the laptop which was sitting on a small round coffee table next to him.

It was then Ramirez asked in a very confused tone,

"What's on here"? The assailant didn't reply and gestured him to look. Ramirez was quickly on the laptop and into the files stored on the hardrive, he scoured a little before clicking on one. His face scrunched up in confusion as he read and watched file after file. He quickly realised why the assailant was doing what he was. He got up to ask him something, but when he did the assailant was gone. He rushed to the door and saw the assailant approaching the end of the hallway.

Ramirez called out to him, "Hey stop! Wait up"! Ramirez tried to chase after, it was then when something happened.

The familiar sound of glass shattering and the sound of a body slumping to the ground made the assailant turn. He saw that Ramirez was slumped against the wall with blood seeping out from his gut. He made an attempt to run towards him, but a second bullet struck him clean in the head killing him instantly. The assailant realised that

Ramirez had been followed.

He could do nothing for him, the priority was to destroy the hardrive. He waited a little before diving low towards the small table, two shots quickly rung out as they pierced the wall behind him. The assailant retrieved the hardrive before doing something foolhardy. He charged low and jumped out of the window as bullets rebounded of his armour as well as the stone wall.

The assailant landed awkwardly, but the pain was something that he could not even think about. He ran down towards the street while bullets poured on to him form every which way. He did what he could to return fire, but he was a fish in a barrel. Eventually he made it out to the open street, running as quickly as he could to whichever alleyway, barely dodging bullets which whistled past him.

There were cars chasing him too and quickly the adrenaline gave way to pain but he was only a few meters away from the river Rhine. He jumped into the air as a bullet from a very powerful rifle struck him across the lower abdomen. He writhed in pain but soon quickly found his way to the bottom of the river, towards the contraption that he had hidden form sight.

Some men appeared on the edge of the river firing into it, but by then the assailant had escaped and was away. He was spent in energy and ideas, it was the first time that he had been ambushed badly like this, now it was certain confiding in anyone but himself was detrimental to his success.

Chapter Thirty: Sanctity

The attempt on the assailant had left him severely wounded. Ramirez was dead he was sure of it; he knew now he was at the mercy of Iron River. There was very little he could do outmanoeuvre him. He had managed to sneak away undetected, but he hadn't got very far, the snow he was now trudging would have given him away but fortunately for him it was dark, and a new spell of snow was falling partially covering his tracks.

There were very few people he could turn to; he was hoping that maybe the cold snow would claim him or maybe he could commit his soul to the river. These thoughts passed in his head as more thick and viscous blood poured from his limbs, it was a miracle that he wasn't bawling out in pain or the fact that he could he even walk. Something within him was unwilling to give up.

Eventually his body succumbed to the tiredness and he fell not that far from a ram, shackled, ageing farm. In that moment he had no care in the world what would become of him, yet there remained in him an ember of guilt clinging on to the very fringes of his life. Slowly but surely due to blood loss and tiredness his eyes closed, and everything faded to black.

It wasn't until till he heard a cockerel squawking and the feeling of the piercing warmth of the morning sunlight, awoke him from his slumber. At first, he was confused was he dead or just hallucinating? It took him awhile to take in his surroundings and to make an assessment as to where he was. He could see that he was confided to a bed. There was a wooden floor beneath him with a trap door close to the wall. A single window and a pair of curtains in front of him were opened allowing the morning sun in. Next to him was a small dresser with an antique oil lamp upon it. Above him were large timbers propping up a roof. It wasn't long before he came to the realisation that he was in a bedroom of sorts in an attic. Then a sense of rapid urgency creeped in, whose bedroom and which house was he in?

He removed his blanket and tried to get out of his bed but stumbled to the ground as something jerked him back, causing the floorboards to creak. He saw his foot was chained to the bed, he tried to undo it but with no success. Then he heard footsteps running up the stairs and it wasn't long before an old, big and burly moustached French man burst through the trap door and appeared before him brandishing a shotgun timidly. The assailant understood that there was very little he could do, the man signalled to the assailant to move back to the bed which he did.

It wasn't long before the Frenchman started raising questions, the assailant understood what he was saying but chose to not to reply. Frustrated by the lack of answers but content with the relative safety of the situation, he relaxed his shotgun to his side as he muttered to himself in French, "What am I going to do with you"?

The assailant turned his attention towards the trap door when he heard another set of footsteps come up stairs, they were slow and very quiet, and before long another figure stood before him. It appeared to be the Frenchman's wife who looked old but was still sprightly for her age. She looked at the Frenchman and they squabbled for a bit; the assailant smiled.

The overpowering smell of cow dung wafted its way through the window and filled the nostrils of assailant. Then he realised where he was in a farm. The man most likely before him was probably a farmer and the women his wife. The women turned to the assailant and began apologizing in French, she removed the shackle tying him to the bed as her husband looked on with caution.

The assailant acknowledged her sympathy by nodding his head in thanks. He placed his hand on the bedpost as he struggled to stand on his feet. The wife signalled her husband to help the assailant up, begrudgingly he agreed.

Over the coming weeks in which the assailant recovered, he gained the trust of the farmer and dispelled little nuggets of information to them through pencil and paper. He was told that the farmer's wife had discovered him by the gate of their farmhouse and that they had brought him into their home. Luckily for him the old farmer was a pretty decent doctor and so was the farmer's wife it was no coincidence, both had been doctors in a past life, so he was told. He knew that their kindness had saved him from an almost certain death. The information that he was dispelling they deserved to know but he also recognized that he had placed them in grave peril.

Therefore, he had decided to leave as soon as possible after he had recovered enough, but not before leaving them something very dear to him as a token of appreciation. The day he left he made sure to make them aware that if anyone was to ask, they knew not of him or of his existence and whatever was to happen they were to never to seek him out. He said his goodbyes and left.

The token was something of a mystery but dear to him and it was a mystery as to why he had chosen to leave it to them. It appeared as a token of goodwill, but it felt as if it was something more.

Chapter Thirty-One: Frustration

Iron River had let the assailant slip much to the old tsar's disappointment. The president had summoned Iron River to ascertain as to why he had failed. The rain was pouring in Moscow and the low bearing ominous clouds were filled with rumbling thunder. As the rain grew in intensity with the rapturous thunder a small inconspicuous black car entered the rear of the presidential palace. The door was slowly opened by a frightened presidential guard. Out steeped the bitter cold, his face was not to amused. His displeasure was justifiable given that his attention had been diverted from preparations for a final assault.

He made sure that his frustration was made clear through every footstep he took. Normally it would take all but two minutes for Iron River to walk from the entrance to the president's office. Yet today he made sure it lasted a whole ten minutes. By the time he reached the door in which the president was waiting for him, he decided to sit in a chair a few meters away from the door. There he sat waiting for the president himself come and receive him.

Eventually growing discontent with the continued tardiness Iron River, the president stepped out of his office in search of him. Much to his annoyance he saw him sitting rather comfortably with a wry smile on his face. He ushered him into his office with a face full of rage. Eventually both men were seated in his office.

Unlike the president of the USA the Russian president was aware of the details of Iron River's exploits. The conversation began in earnest, the president rose from his seat, his voice slowly one word at a time built up into a tirade. He let lose a whole host offensive slurs and it did not seize until he had exhausted every word in the dictionary, he could use to offend Iron River.

This burst of anger was from the drop in his approval ratings and nothing else.

During that whole outburst Iron River did not flinch, speak or move, the president had assumed that his words had pierced him somehow. How wrong he was, at the end of his tirade Iron River smirked wickedly.

He rose from his seat and stared down towards the president with his venomous eyes, exhaling and inhaling slowly. His voice rose gradually from his throat until the words unfurled from his tongue. He spoke in a such a spine-tingling manner it felt as though a mountain was thundering down upon you. Every word conveyed his unmistakeable power and it almost immediately had the president trembling in cold sweat.

"Romanov son of Vasilyev son of Krakhov, know I am the kingmaker". With each sentence the distance between Iron River and the president grew smaller and smaller as his voice grew louder and louder.

"I am the constructor of crowns; I am the builder of fearsome men and destroyer of nations. I hold the will of all Russians in the palm of my right hand. In the other is the furious winter tide, forged in unmistakable, unrelenting, unforgiving Iron blood".

He inhaled once more "Know that I make our nation's most terrible leaders look weak and feeble. And those yet to come will come trembling at my feet".

He inhaled again, "Know that hell has no place for my wickedness, and I am the devil of these lands".

He pointed at his chest before he spoke again, "In this frail body which is hampered with old age there is a river which flows. Know it is the same river that carves this land. No material, no man here or anywhere can stop it".

He pointed to his head before he spoke once more, "Know that in this mind there are plans upon plans for the destruction of you and your family. You are a chess piece that I move at my pleasure, so easily can you be replaced. Not the strength of the Douma not even the forces which you command will be able to help you".

He was a few steps away from the president now, "I am the unbreakable cog in a machine that will continue to rumble on for millennia to come. Know Romanov I am the Iron River least you forget".

The president was not boisterous or confident whatever false sense of victory he had was quickly gone. He knew as he looked into the eyes of the Iron River that he would not be who he was today without his help. His courage had whimpered away at the sound of the Iron River's words. Now he was bent and knuckled under the pressure of Iron River. When Iron River had finished speaking, he grabbed the president by his collar and brought him close, "When I have accomplished my task at hand I will foresee to your suffering". Iron River dropped his collar walked to the door slammed it and left.

Chapter Thirty-Two: Case-Closed

In order to avoid any more mishaps or prying eyes, Iron River had devised a plan to deviate and finally place to rest, any theories that the other countries may have had about what was going on.

The first thing he did was to dispel any myth about the Russians committing attacks on American soil. So, he concocted a fictitious terrorist organisation with real brainwashed people with the most far reaching views. He called the organisation 'Heterodox' a so-called anarchy group with singular goal of causing chaos around the world, placing the same group right wing Dark Star mentioned under it. There arose some difficulty the nature of the attacks meant each one had to be attributed to one another in a conclusive way. It was easy to sway the opinions of the Americans to sincerely believe what he was spewing out. The French, Chinese, English,

Pakistanis and Indians eventually came around to his way of thinking as for the Russians well that was simple to deal with.

Iron River knew that he had to place a significant paper trail of concrete evidence, these attacks had to look like that they had taken years to plan. So, he made sure to sow evidence in every which place he could find.

The issue of explaining the conglomerate of men that had died in New York including his mutual acquaintance of Dark Star was linked to Heterodox with fictitious evidence. With this he managed to ease the qualms of the intelligence services in America.

There also remained the nagging issue of the assailant who was captured and had escaped, which had to be answered. The answer to this problem was given through a cadaver with a self-inflicted gun wound. Iron River had made sure that the agencies of America would find it with all the incriminating evidence like the costume and documents of fake plans. He made sure to link this body to the attacks in the USA and the world and made him the leader of the anarchist group. This was enough for the Americans and others to stop investigating.

With the Gentleman he covered his death by using his own agents and operatives to make it look like that he had died of an accidental fire.

Then there was the issue of the Mountain. The attack upon him was in full view of the public so to deceive them he; First, he made sure to adjust the coroner's report to fit his narrative. Then he made sure to destroy any evidence linking him or the other patriarchs with one another as he was aware of the habits of the Mountain. He liked to keep incriminating evidence about him and the other patriarchs. Finally, he made the investigation appear as though the Mountain was an agent who had died in the line of duty fighting the fictitious anarchist group. This was by using his many undercover agents in the French police and the French intelligence agencies.

The last part of this mess he had to sort out was something that he had created. Ramirez the pesky FBI agent who had discovered the whereabouts of the assailant, and who was now dead had to be addressed. It would not be long before the FBI would be questioning his whereabouts. There was also the issue of this girl who had seen too much, his agents had alerted him of her. He knew that she had only confided in Ramirez, so for now he decided to let her live.

As for Ramirez he would remain missing till he could resolve the issue of the assailant. He had assumed incorrectly that the issues had all but been resolved in truth it could not have been further from the truth. Sure, he could change the narrative to suit his own needs, but he could not predict or even control the story to come.

His trickery, guile and cunning had served him well, but he was to face an adversary that was not easily overcome. An adversary who had wiped out most of his competitors with relative ease. He had one fleeting attempt and it had ended in failure. Next time the assailant would be at full strength and prepared, after killing him only then would be able to finally say 'case closed'.

Chapter Thirty-Three: Last Message

A tall, righteous woman walked swiftly down a hall with her right hand clasped on to a letter. She passed one set of doors after the other stopping at the door marked with the number two hundred and one. She knocked just once and waited; the door slowly creped open as tired eyes looked on inquisitively. The tall women extended out her hands and soft hands took the letter from her and she left. The door closed, and those soft hands opened the strange letter slowly and neatly.

The eyes became transfixed on every word. This letter did not start with dear, hi or hello.

This letter in case it reaches you should be considered my last. In the event you do not hear from me or see me again. Do not attempt to follow up on me or my wellbeing, if you do it will place you in a peril that I will not be able to protect you from. I know you have questions that I have never answered that which you have desired to know. I ask of you to quell these curiosities to these questions as their answers must remain under a veil of shadows. I wish I could tell you everything, but the risk is too great. One day when all is said is done you may finally be able to discover all that hid from you. Until that day if someone does come knocking please say you don't know me.

I have made all the necessary arrangements for your financial needs and other such obligations. Our relationship must be buried to the deepest part of your mind. The threat of you being discovered is too high and you being caught is unacceptable. I place what remaining trust I have with you. I have taught you whatever I could, there is nothing that remains.

I know that you are strong, and I know that you are wise but grow wiser and grow stronger. Wiser and stronger than I will ever be, wherever I have failed to make amends be better than me. Until then don't find me, don't return home. Kill all your links to me, forget me, move on and burn this letter.

At first the soft eyes and face swelled with confusion, then with anger. Then it gave way to tears which rolled down the cheek dropping until they fell upon the letter. Eventually the paper burned away with tears as the ink faded away.

Chapter Thirty-Four: Turbulent Mind

After the explosive outburst against the president Iron River had returned to his decrepit home. He was contemplating what he had just said to the president, he wondered if the president had any courage to stop him or to even stand up to him. Sure, he had shown some courage by insulting him but as soon as he spoke the president had no response, where was his voice then?

Something that bothered him more than that was the fact that he had chosen him to succeed the previous as the next president. He felt as though his judgement was not sound, that it was becoming too indecisive. He questioned as to what weakness made him choose such a weak leader. He paced himself in the living room of his home and stopped to study the embers that slowly fell from the fire that he had lit. He watched it burn and spit, his eyes looked deeper into the fiery cavernous pit and for but a moment his eyes filled with sadness, it quickly dissipated. He looked away from the fire and looked to his left and then to his right hand and looked away at the sight of some old scars. Something pained him something that he had hidden away for a long time.

Within his mind raged a conflict of duty and something else it was reflected in the way he adorned his home. The home of Iron was barren only the essentials were ever present. No paintings or pictures hung from the halls. The only decorative part was the Russian eagle at the front door and the Russian flag which hung from a flagpole outside. As well as a neat and welcoming office filled by the warmth of an indoor fire. It was almost as if the outside of his home represented his patriotism to his nation as a façade and inside past the many dark hallways and rooms, was the inner most sanctum of his mind a complicated and conflicted man.

Duty, honour and pride is what compelled him to do the tasks presented to him. It was more important than anything because like he said to the president, he carried the 'will of the Russian people'. He could not abandon his post not ever, not even after his death. In his mind the conflicting morals of good and bad played out again and again. Giving up seemed so easy.

As he battled himself in one half of his mind, the other battled the man who confidently stood challenging him. This was a man who was not entirely conflicted. He was not consumed by his plaguing thoughts. He unlike everyone else knew why he was doing what he was doing. There was no conflict there was no judgment as to whether he did good or bad. He had been judged in the eyes of others without the proof of evidence, there was no justice for him when he yearned for it. Justice was but a loose term for all those men that he had killed, they had no understanding of it. They were not bound by it they only cared for money power and greed. He had enough of labels, enough of people saying what he could and could not do. He would carry the response to every person whose strike went unanswered he would be the hand of justice. If it cost him his life it was a price that he was more than willing to pay.

The worlds eyes had been deceived by the words of Iron River they had believed every word he had fed them. Dark Star was a patriot, the Mountain a French hero and the Gentleman a poor man who had been consumed by fire. They bought all of it every damn piece of it. There secrets would die with them and the only two men who had any idea what they were would be, was the assailant and Iron River. Two sides of a coin locked in conflict that no one knew about.

Chapter Thirty-Five: Reckoning

In the cold and bitter land of Russia Iron River bided his time and developed all sorts of plans. In the southern half of France there was the assailant preparing for his very last battle. Both men were equally determined, neither being able to stop the other so far.

By killing Dark Star, the Mountain and the Gentlemen who really stood in the way of Iron River expect the assailant. Those men he had killed had been nothing but false friends to the Iron River and he had done him a favour.

The assailant did not know any better his mind was filled with rage and it was clouded with revenge. One brush of death was not good enough, he would continue to persevere regardless the personal cost he had to endure, to finish what he had started.

Iron River was fuelled not with rage but a quiet confident calm. He had seen how close he could get to the assailant, but this was through another person. He had seen how because of traps his enemies were dead. He had seen how they had turned against them and how they had been turned on their heads to the assailant's advantage. One thing he knew without a shadow of doubt was that the assailant was wounded he must have suffered when he had attacked him. He knew that it would be easier now surely, but he could not take any chances.

The issue remained for the Iron River how was he to find him? His men had been searching for him across Southern France to no avail. He had no idea as to where he was now, if he had maybe he could've ended it quickly and quietly.

The assailant had made his way to the extreme end of the south coast of France, he was south west of the city of Cannes staring at the Mediterranean Sea. The moon was glowing brightly, and it shimmered in the slow rocking waves. He was for the moment trying to sleep but he couldn't as he had not completely healed from the wounds, he had sustained from the attack at the apartment.

All the others had succumbed easily to him, Iron River however was entirely different he was much more careful. He made sure to leave no trace of his existence after anything he did, officially he did not exist he was ghost in Russia. These were the problems that the assailant faced, then the side note something which made the task seem almost impossible to him was the size of Russia, Iron River could be anywhere. So, he sat for the last time on French soil, looked once again at the locket closed and gripped it tight and rose to set off down the coast heading somewhere.

Iron River was sitting in the cold with a dimly lit light looking at some papers. The information was something very important to him. It had arrived to him through an aide of his situated in France it was all the information that Ramirez had gathered on the individual that he had termed 'anomaly'. With that was all the information the Dark Star had, including the details of the failed operation at Bodie and the attack in New York. He also had all the information that the Gentleman and the Mountain had collected up until their deaths. With this information he was now certain as to where to find the assailant.

Chapter Thirty-Six: Hydra

My recollection of the last events is a bit hazy I can't surmise the exact fate of the assailant but from what I am able to conclude there were three stories. I know not if any of them are true.

The first of these stories I was told was something to behold, it was filled daring escapes, numerous flamboyant explosion and lion like courage. Yet ultimately the ending was tragic.

It began as soon as Iron River returned from the eventful meeting with the Russian president. The assailant had been staying at some old, friendly, French farming, couple's home. He had stayed there for several weeks due to the injuries he had sustained at the apartment, but they had now adequately healed for him to get out. There was no certainty in his conviction anymore he had just had a brush with the doors of death. Whatever he was planning to do would be his last plan and everything had to be taken into consideration.

Meanwhile a much flustered and agitated Iron River was frantically searching for him in every nook and crevice that he knew of. After several weeks the search stopped, and he tracked back to Moscow to re-evaluate his strategy. He studied his enemy's methods with precisional detail analysing every mistake he had made. He looked at the other patriarchs and as to how they had met their fates. He examined what footage he had of the assailant, he looked at times, dates and location. Through several of hours of dedicated focus he eventually knew what he had not done, and that was to let the assailant slip on his own accord.

The things that he understood was, if he was to pursue the evidence planted by the assailant it would lead into a trap. If he was to remain in the hopes of defending his castle he would be overwhelmed and to send his own men into the fray would certainly get them killed. The solution that Iron River came up with was risky, he was to place himself in harm's way but not openly nor discreetly but somewhere in between or at least that's what it would seem.

By now the assailant was in Russia and was searching for Iron River in the hopes he could score a quick and fatal blow. Before him was the enormous difficulty in tracking Iron River. He searched and searched until the defence of the fatherland day, only then did an opportunity arise for an occasion to deal such a blow.

Unbeknownst to the assailant it was nothing short of a spider's trap. He had discovered a set of dignitaries who were going to be present at a night-time parade in Moscow and one such name drew the attention of the assailant, Grigory Vasiliyev. The newspaper had stated that this man was a businessman from the city of Kazan and there was a photo attached to the name. The assailant instantly recognized the photo. He knew that this was Iron River he was hopeful that Iron River had made a hapless mistake. He began preparing, cleaning his equipment readying his armour making sure of the routes and maps.

Then came the day, watching rom the rooftops of an abandoned building he spotted him through the scope of his rifle, but being smarter decided to wait until his victim was in a quiet, isolated place. He watched him place wreaths and observe a minute silence, shortly after he was in a car heading down a small narrow street. The assailant followed with his scope till he could no more and made his way towards his target, placing some devices around him and his target.

Eventually he was laying down again with Iron River's head in his cross-sight. From the rooftops of another building he inhaled in the cold air and pulled the trigger, closing his eyes hoping upon hope that this man was dead. When he opened them, his eyes filled with dread, the target was still standing he had missed. He reloaded to fire again, but rapid gunfire burst open against his concealed position, he was pinned. The assailant quickly slung his rifle over his shoulder and made a break for it. His armour pinged as bullets ricocheted off it. He slid behind cover and returned fire carelessly, the bullets connected with flesh and bone killing some men.

The assailant kept firing till his ammunition had finished and was left with nothing but his melee weapons. He had been duped and corned, he mustered his tattered courage and was just about to jump over his cover and charge one last time, until he heard a voice.

"Come out we have you cornered you have nowhere to run", the assailant hesitated but realising his situation he slowly stepped out and looked to see the face of a very pleased man.

"Now finally I have you", the man chuckled as he walked slowly over until he was about ten yards away.

"The pain you have exacted on everyone comes with a price, a price you are going to pay". The assailant looked straight on at Iron River as he spoke, increasing his grip on his blade.

"You have caused so many problems I should be in awe as to the way you have managed to evade me for so long, but it doesn't, merely talking to you doesn't quell my insatiable thirst for vengeance. People like you just need to die, yet there remains a question unanswered, who are you"?

The assailants mask lifted to reveal a face filled with pent up rage, Iron River squinted to look and the staggered back in shock and in sheer terror told his men to fire. The assailants mask immediately collapsed and he charged towards Iron River as heavy rounds pierced his body. Iron River ran but the blade quickly pierced his flesh as he gasped for his last breaths. Iron River looked at the assailant with eyes packed with fear as the assailant reached out his hand so that Iron River could see, and he whispered, "Your secret dies with you and me".

In the hand was a detonator and as the assailant pressed it the area lit up with a terrifying explosion. There the story ended with mangled corpses, jagged steel, crumpled rubble and secrets.

The second account I was told was brazen. The assailant had understood that the bump in the road of vengeance was Iron River. He understood the difficulty of the task that had been presented to him, so he decided to do something that would surely get his attention. He decided to pen a letter directly to him with a time, date and place, he could not be sure that the letter would reach him, but he wrote it anyway.

Privet, Mr Zhukov, I am the man who you have been

searching for. The one that has been causing you so much pain and anger. I have tried to find you, but it seems that it is proving to be very difficult. So, I suggest an alternative why don't you come and find me? I know that your intentions are clear you wish for me dead, I will be happy to oblige. I hope to settle this amicably with you and if you absolutely need to, bring as many men you feel like.

The letter travelled through the various sorting offices before arriving at the FSI headquarters. It landed into the hands of a secretary who made sure to pass it on to Iron River. He was in his office at home sifting through some papers, his associate had placed the letter on a pile of folders and binders, at first Iron River paid no attention to it as he was busy reading some files. After he stopped examining the files, he turned his attention to the letter. He picked up and examined it carefully, then he reached for his letter opener and sliced open the letter. The letter was unfolded, and his eyes examined each word intently.

Upon finishing the letter, he smirked, how foolish did this man think he was, this was surely a ploy. He was not as stupid or as careless as the rest, a location of his choosing. He chuffed almost exclaiming who does he think he is? Does he not know who I am? Still there was the small possibility the assailant was giving up and there might be an opportunity to end this once and for all. He paced around his desk considering how he could possibly manipulate the situation to his advantage. There was very little time to deliberate a decision, the assailant had set a deadline.

Iron River was slightly caught up in the sheer bravado he had mustered to send him a letter, even after all the things that he done. He had a few hunches as to why he had sent him this letter, other than the obvious that he wanted him dead. Was he tired of running and fighting? Did he finally want to come out of the shadows? Or was it something that he could possibly not know about, something that he held deep inside something that he would never know? The hand of the clock continued to move as Iron River continued explore what he could do? Realising that the assailant had given him a time constraint, he decided to go with as many men as he could.

Like always it was dark, the cold winter had fully set in. A black car had arrived into an undisclosed pitch-dark, flat cavernous area. It was surrounded by mountains, very little could be seen other than the dim moonlight shining against black, silvery, rocks. From the car emerged Iron River or so it seemed wearing a black felt trench coat. He had a scarf tightly wrapped around his neck; it covered the lower half of his chin. The figure at first looked around searching for something then eventually called out in Russian,

"I'm here you piece of shit, show yourself"! His

breath lingered in the cold air; it fell quiet after his echoes had reverberated around. He was waiting for a reply of some sorts yet there was nothing, so he called out again, "I'm here show yourself"!

Unbeknownst to him there on ridge was the assailant lying in wait like a lion in the brush, staring down the scope of his rifle. The man he had come to kill was before him, surely now it could end. With a slight squeeze of the trigger the bullet was let loose from its cartridge and jettisoned forward towards it target. The eyes of the assailant remained fixed on his target all the way. The bullet arrived smashing into flesh and bone shattering it into many bloody pieces. The body almost in slow motion came crashing to the ground. The assailant cocked the gun was once more and stared down his rifle's scope to make sure that his target was down.

A sense of relief passed over his shoulders, yet he remained sceptical. He could have walked away, but something dragged him back. He slung his rifle on his back and made his way down from the ridge releasing loose gravel as he came down. He trudged carefully examining the other ridges one by one. He neared the body paying no attention to the remains of the head, there was only thing he was interested in, the left hand.

He knelt to examine it, he reached into one of his pockets to pull out a small flashlight. He shone the light onto the hand, and as soon as he saw it, he dropped it realising that it was not Iron River. His attention quickly turned to raising his shield it was in the process of forming when unexpectedly he heard a phone ringing. He immediately looked to the man who was dead on the floor and opened his jacket to reveal a beeping suicide vest. He placed the still forming shield in front of him and in an instant a thunderous explosion flung him ten meters back. The explosion agitated a huge amount of dust and rock meshed with human flesh into the air. For a moment making it impossible to see.

The vision of the assailant became blurry as he slowly staggered to his feet. His head was spinning all over the place, when the dust had begun to settle, some of his senses began to return to him. He placed his shield in front of him, struggling to stand up then slowly like an infant he ran to the ridge, but every step he took tracer rounds lit up his view disorienting him further. Some rounds punched into him knocking him right and left. Other rounds sent plumes of dust kicking into the air. He fired back with his pistols from wherever he could see incoming fire.

Then came the sound of screeching rockets the first just missed him, the second struck the dirt releasing a plume of dust on the very far left-hand side. The third hit blew up in front of him knocking him down for good. The assailant could not get up now as one of his legs would not move. He quickly found out there was a piece of steel lodged in his leg pinning it to the ground and his right arm had become limp and was bleeding.

The gunfire and explosions settled, as the assailant lay there writhing in pain. The sound of footsteps approached and through the settling dust came Iron River and his men. He reached for his guns, but they had been knocked from him. Iron River looked at him and then asked him to remove his mask. At first, he hesitated then he undid the locks binding his mask to his suit.

Iron River looked carefully; horror was the first emotion that became transfixed on his face. In a panic he reached for his gun swinging it to face the assailant. The assailant extended his left hand to reveal a grenade. The gun went off and so did the grenade. The bullet killed the assailant instantly, but he did not die without leaving Iron River a painful reminder. The grenade had ripped Iron River's left leg to pieces as a result he had to have it amputated. The assailant perished into the sands of history along with his pain and torment. Whilst the man he had come to kill lived on with a painful reminder.

The last story was filled with blind rage, sadness and gumption. The assailant had already seen enough and done enough, he had dragged someone into a mess of his doing and that person was dead. He was still licking his wounds from the attack at the apartment. Something in his mindset had changed, seeing someone who had done no wrong die before him had altered him. As he sat staring into the waters of the Mediterranean, he contemplated whether it would be easier just to die. The hours of the night ticked till finally he decided to end it all. He tied a large rock to his feet stared into the deep waters and jumped. The black water swallowed him up. He closed his eyes as the rock slowly sank deeper and deeper.

The eyes however would not remain closed, something swelled inside him. His eyes burst open and his arms and legs began to fight back. The urge of survival was coursing through his blood, the rock however was still fixed to his leg. He frantically tried to loosen the knot, whilst precious air escaped from his lungs. Eventually the knot was undone, and the rock sank to the abyssal depths of the sea. He yielded whatever strength he had left in him and surged upwards as fast as he could. He was losing his air too fast, salty water began pouring into his mouth and nose, he was drowning. It was at that point when his vision began to blur, and his arms began to weaken moving closer to the surface of the sea above him. Like a dead hand from the grave his head reached out from the sea and he gasped for air. He stayed in the water for a while catching his breath eventually making it slowly and laboriously to the shore.

From the abysmal plains of suicide, he rose a new man with a solitary goal. Kill the Iron river. Whatever the cost, no matter where he had to go to do it, he would kill Iron River. He shook his mind from those grimacing thoughts and memories of pain and fixed his mind onto a new unshakable determination.

He mounted his bike and rode quickly under the waning light of the moon to the nearest marina in Marseille. He arrived and made his way to the dock, unbeknownst to anyone he had hid a submersible ship of his own construction, under the waves beneath the wooden docks. He had used this sturdy and fast ship to reach many of his destinations.

It wasn't long before he and his bike were inside of it. He set of from the south coast of France under the new rising sun. His journey led him to pass through the strait of Bonifacio between the islands of Corsica and Sardinia, soon the ship passed into the strait of Messina, the shortest point between the Italian mainland and the island of Sicily. From there the ship passed into the Ionian Sea and travelled North East. Sailing between the island of Zakynthos and the Peloponnese peninsula. It went under the Rion Antirion bridge and into the gulf of Corinth. He travelled under the cover of darkness covering huge distances. The canal of Corinth proved difficult given the inability to manoeuvre much but the ship crammed through.

It raced passed the islands of Attica peninsula and passed through the plethora of South Aegean Islands and into the Aegean Sea. By now several days had passed, the assailant was resting in the day and travelling by night. He sailed into the Dardanelles and into the sea of Manarma before existing through the Bosporus and into the Black sea. The ship travelled slowly through these waters avoiding the Russian tankers and military vessels operating in the area.

Eventually the shores of the Russian Caucuses appeared. He rested his ship on a ledge under the black waters of the Black Sea. He disembarked from his ship with his bike attached to a float and him clinging to it before it surfaced. Under the cover of the dark he made his way to shore and made his camp and slept concealed from prying eyes. It took him but a week to traverse the waters but now lay ahead of him the daunting task of travelling through Russia.

He had no assurances Iron River was even in Russia, there was no guarantee that wherever here traversed in Russia was safe. There was very little he was certain of. Rage nonetheless fuelled him forward with little regard for the dangers that may become apparent. Iron River was nowhere in Russia. He was in a frigid barren area, in the most northern of northern territories of Norway.

Nestled between some tall evergreen trees, a small timber house releasing smoke from a chimney drifted into the wind. Within there was Iron River sitting near the amber glow of a timber fire. He was sat in a sturdy chair examining a picture, a memory of some remnant life of old. Something which had long since been forgotten to him. He seemed to be in a sombre, pondering, mood as if he was stuck in some thought.

Little did it matter, the rage filled assailant pressed on, by night he traversed the land and in the day he rested. First, he passed through Sochi, then onwards towards the city of Krasnodar and resting on the first day in the city of Rostov-on-don. On the second day he made it to Volgograd, by the third he crossed into Saratov. On day four he was in Voronezh and by the fifth he was in Moscow.

It was only on the sixth night did the carnage begin; the assailant had readied his armour his weapons and munitions ready for one last battle. In the night he entered the place from which he had heard Iron River concocted his plans.

He was on the borders of a compound somewhere on the outskirts of Moscow, he jumped over the wall which surrounded the property. Then it began, the first man to fall was a sentry patrolling near some vehicles, he made quick work by slicing his throat. Then the next fell with a quick and silent shot to the head. He worked his way around the exits removing one sentry after another. The kill count rapidly racketed up. Then he made his way into the large building located in the centre of the compound. He blew open the door, two hapless Russian sentries looked on and frantically raised their guns to shoot, they were quickly put down.

More men began to pour into the many halls and staircases. He mercilessly shot them down as some stood and fired, tearing up seat cushions, splintering wood and shattering glass. Yet they all fell one after the other the numbers became points, twenty-seven, thirty-two, thirty-nine, forty-five and so on and so forth. He had

slaughtered as many as seventy men, but he was only

here for one man, Iron River. He made his way down the

longest hall towards the grandest room, once again he

blew opened the doors. He gritted his teeth and released a

hail of bullets without a care given to look. Once the

paper, dust and wood began to settle he realised no-one

was there.

After all this effort and all the dead men lying

slumped on the ground, why wasn't he here? He heard a

faint laughter coming from the hall and set off to

investigate. There in the hall was one of the men lying

slumped to the wall bubbling blood out from his mouth

slowly, laughing faintly.

"All this effort and you couldn't get to him" he

chortled. "You want to know where he his? You know

the funny thing is none of us knows where he goes". The

man chuckled a few times again before his life slipped

away.

The assailant incensed frantically searched each room. He turned over tables tapped the wall for any secret area. Until eventually he arrived back at Iron River's office. There he saw the distinct holes made by his bullets, but there was a certain cluster of them which had given way to form a larger hole.

Through the darkness of the hole he could just about make out the faint glimmer of steel. He ventured forward and to find out what it was. He slowly tore away at the surrounding wall, each piece he took off revealed more of the steel. Eventually it became apparent as to what it was, a safe. There was something Iron River had been hiding even from his own men. The safe was securely locked and was protected by a passcode. It wasn't long before anomaly had gone off in search of tools to crack it open.

He scrounged around the compound in search of tools

and eventually he came across an assortment of them including a hammer drill with bits, a carbon dioxide fire extinguisher and an ordinary hammer. He made a hole near the lock using the drill and poured in the contents of the extinguisher into it, then he struck it several times and it broke away.

The door swivelled open, he peered inside, and his eyes fixed themselves to the object inside. It wasn't money, gold or anything else except a tattered, old, black leather, book with fading gold margins. He placed the book on the desk and flicked the first page open revealing photos of someone possibly dear to Iron River, they looked old given the attire of the person in the photo. The eyes of the assailant began to race through each page examining each photo, date and every bit of text, finally finding the place where Iron River was.

There was a photo of what looked like a wood cabin located between some pine trees. He studied this photo carefully it was the only one with no people on it. He flipped it over to examine the other side, on there was a note addressed to Iron River.

Dear Zhukov, the cabin that you found is perfect, I know you haven't had time as of late to see it, so I took a photo for you. I hope to see you soon. Love from M.K.

On the side it was marked with an address Sirma Norway. Rummaging through some more in the book he stumbled upon a small map, it was a little tattered and creased but still readable. Before he left, he torched the building burning every corpse and everything within it. Now, he had everything he needed to finally kill Iron River.

Mr Zhukov was sitting enjoying dinner alone by the fire on the oak table. The sun had set under the horizon, the sky was dark with the exceptions of a few green and blueish flares of a faint aurora. The snow surrounding the timber home was deep and only one path was clear. The sound of faint footsteps of Iron River's men crunching against the snow as they patrolled the property, whispered in the wind.

Far out on a hill red eyes watched through night vison binoculars. The assailant was here, Iron River was none the wiser. The assailant filled with no humanity slowly trekked closer towards the timber home. Through the scope of his rifle the first few men fell silently and quickly.

With the rest he gutted and slit their throats until all of Iron River's men were dead. He walked down the only path clear of snow towards the door. It was then the nagging shroud of doubt travelled up Iron River's spine. The door swung open, there in the frame stood the figure of a man who had caused him so much trouble.

The man who had never spoken raised his gun fired once and once again. The first hit the heart the second on the head, now Iron River was dead.

ISBN:9781695241220

Printed in Poland
by Amazon Fulfillment
Poland Sp. z o.o., Wrocław

50383240R00169